HEART OF THE COTSWOLDS: ENGLAND

A LOVE ABROAD B&B ROMANCE

M. L. BUCHMAN

Buchman Bookworks

SIGN UP FOR M. L. BUCHMAN'S NEWSLETTER TODAY

and receive:
Release News
Free Short Stories
a Free Starter Library

Do it today. Do it now.
www.mlbuchman.com/newsletter

Main Flight

Pure Heat

Full Blaze

Hot Point

Flash of Fire

Wild Fire

Smokejumpers

Wildfire at Dawn

Wildfire at Larch Creek

Wildfire on the Skagit

Delta Force

Main Flight

Target Engaged

Heart Strike

Wild Justice

Henderson's Ranch

Nathan's Big Sky

Love Abroad B&B

Heart of the Cotswolds: England

Where Dreams

Where Dreams are Born

Where Dreams Reside

Where Dreams Are of Christmas

Where Dreams Unfold

Where Dreams Are Written

<u>**Eagle Cove**</u>

Return to Eagle Cove

Recipe for Eagle Cove

Longing for Eagle Cove

Keepsake for Eagle Cove

Deities Anonymous

Cookbook from Hell: Reheated

Saviors 101

<u>**Dead Chef**</u>

Swap Out!

One Chef!

Two Chef!

<u>**SF/F Titles**</u>

The Nara Reaction

Monk's Maze

The Me and Elsie Chronicles

Strategies for Success

Managing Your Inner Artist / Writer

Don't miss a thing! Get a free starter library!

www.mlbuchman.com

CHAPTER 1

Aaron struck gold. His favorite table, tucked deep in the corner past the big stone fireplace that dominated The Queen's Guard pub, freed up just as he came in.

Extra bonus—he'd question the height of his standards some other day—the departing local had left behind a copy of the *Daily Mirror.* Not the most scurrilous of the English scandal sheets, but not exactly *The Times* either. It offered the perfect amount of camp for a Friday afternoon. A pint of the local Donnington ale and he was content.

Bridget would know that he'd not be ready for his beef-and-mustard ale pie until he was at least halfway down the pint.

As always, he toasted the owner's old dog before taking the first sip. After three months here, Snoop—short for Snoop Doggy Dogg, a knee-high Cavalier King Charles Spaniel—barely bothered to acknowledge Aaron's arrival from his pillow close by the fire-warm hearth. It was a nice change. For most of his first month here, Snoop had delivered a sharp reprimand every time Aaron entered the pub.

After a long day of work, the Queen's Guard had become Aaron's retreat of choice and not only because they rented him a

1

cheap room close under the third floor eaves and served a fine breakfast.

The pub itself dated back two hundred years before the Puritans had landed on Plymouth Rock in Massachusetts, yet it was far from the oldest building in the village of Fosse-on-the-Wold. The trademark yellow Cotswold limestone was dusted gray by its centuries as a pub. The massive beams always made him duck, even though experience had taught him they were several inches clear of his six-foot-one, except the one by the back corner table—something he never managed to remember when crowding forced him to sit so far from his favorite spot by the hearth.

The tables and chairs were by far the newest element of the furnishings, and they predated the American Civil War.

Yet despite its age, there was something about the place that felt brand new, as if the pub had been born the moment he walked into. It had a vitality that he'd lost in himself a year ago. Tonight it took a hard effort, but he managed to once more close off that past and tamp it down—hard.

The pub was abuzz with casual afternoon chatter. Not a single massive flat-screen TV in sight. Though that didn't keep the Brits from their sports talk.

"Oy, did you hear what they're paying those blokes what play for Manchester United? It's just kickin' a ball up and down the field. Me and the lads done that plenty 'urselves."

Yeah, the three blokes with beer guts were going to show David Beckham and Bobby Charlton a move or two.

The phrase "...that mess in Afghanistan..." caught his attention and he did his best to slam that door closed. He used to care, but didn't any longer. Honestly, he didn't. He forced himself to listen to another table.

"I heard tell that Nelly is going out with that bloke from Bourton."

"Naw, she's taken up with that gypsy she met at the Stow horse fair last November. She's been seeing him on the sly all along don't y'know."

Good luck to Nelly. The local gypsies were a rough lot. Their biannual horse fair and gathering—especially of those of marriageable age—typically shut down Stow-on-the-Wold for several days. He'd been warned to avoid it and, after a brief afternoon of seeing for himself, decided that the locals weren't having him on. The Horse Fair was a good time to not be in Stow.

A man came in, haggard, burned-out homeless. Blank eyes, clothes that even the dump wouldn't want, looking like a stray breeze would take the beggar down. Bridget zeroed in to shoo him off—except she didn't.

"Manfred, it's so good to see you getting out again at long last. We're so sorry for your loss of Matilda. She was always one of our favorites."

He teared up and patted her hand as she escorted him to a table on the far side of the pub. Hal had come out from the bar and was there to offer his condolences as well. Even Snoop went over for a visit.

Aaron didn't feel put out when Hal actually delivered the pint to the man's table rather than expecting him come up to the bar. Aaron had forgotten about small towns during his decade in the military. God but he loved them. They were places where people knew each other. That chance had led him to Fosse-on-the-Wold still amazed him.

Page Two of the *Daily Mail* had a brilliant piece about the Corgi spy dogs that had been infiltrated into the Queen's entourage during the Cold War by Margaret Thatcher during one of her off-again periods with the Royals. The paper was the perfect excuse for clandestine observation of the local birds flocking through.

British English had its uses. Maybe only rude blokes thought of English women as "birds" anymore, but they appeared in such a wonderful variety of leggy brunettes and blondes, especially the blondes. England had trended back to long hair while America was still deeply ensconced in bobs and severe jawline cuts. British women let it grow long, flowing down their backs in soft waves that were truly a joy to watch go by. He'd always been partial to long hair.

He almost missed the blonde's entrance because he was deep in an article on the documented ghosts of Nether Swell Manor, which lay just over the hill and down in the next valley from Fosse-on-the-Wold. He noticed her because of her stillness. Bridget crisscrossed to deliver meals and kindness in equal proportions. A family of Germans moved awkwardly around her still form to either side.

Aaron took a sip of his beer as an excuse to keep watching while she surveyed the room.

She didn't walk like a Brit. Brits had a laziness…no, an ease to their walk. Out here in the country, hurry simply wasn't a part of the daily routine. Even a Londoner down on a whirlwind holiday didn't move with the sharp alacrity of an American. And even among Americans, few moved the way this one did.

Tall, he liked tall. Blonde, no complaints from him. Unlike the soft cascades of British hair, hers lay in a smooth sheet as perfectly controlled as her dancer's posture. Her dress—he still wasn't used to the word frock—was made of fine material and far too fancy for The Queen's Guard. The afternoon sunlight shone through the door from behind, which hid her face in shadow and left it up to the imagination. But it cast just enough light to silhouette without revealing through her summery clothes. Very trim. Aaron definitely liked trim.

For a moment, he was afraid that she'd change her mind and duck away, but she visibly stiffened her already fortified spine and forged ahead. She scanned the room once, her gaze barely pausing as it passed over him, then she moved to the small table just one closer to the fire from his own. She'd dismissed him as neither important nor threatening—sadly, both true.

For a cold winter's night, hers would be his first choice of a table, but on a warm spring day, he preferred to be out of the direct blast of the fire's heat.

Snoop raised his head from his dog pillow to inspect her carefully. Usually he barked at foreigners, more at Americans than continentals. But he inspected the woman in calm silence with his slightly bulging eyes. Even after he settled his head back down on his paws, he watched the woman and Aaron didn't blame him one bit.

She didn't sit facing the pub, which would have placed her back to him, but rather facing the fire. Once his eyes adjusted, he could see her fine features by the fire's light. The face revealed in firelight didn't disappoint in the slightest.

"Elizabeth," it just came out of him.

She turned to face him; her eyes were green and distinctly cool despite the fire's warmth. "No, Jane."

"Sorry," he shot for a British accent but knew he'd missed it along with his chance to pretend he was the least bit exotic. "You are the spitting image of the portrait of Elizabeth the First there," he pointed at the portrait on the pub's far wall.

She turned away to glance at it for only a moment. Her neck was long and elegant, perhaps the best feature on a beautiful woman.

Even more than the portrait, she might be Cate Blanchett when she played Elizabeth in the films. He'd seen almost every film Cate had done—even the romancy things.

"Jane Tully," she repeated flatly, not giving him enough to place any accent. She turned away, offering up her profile for further study.

If he were to shape her face in stone, it would have to be a warm stone to go with the cool features. But the ruddiness of the western Cotswold limestone wouldn't suit her any better than the gold of the eastern. Maybe she *would* be served well by the cool white of an alabaster marble that—

"Don't you have a paper to read?" She didn't even turn from the fire to speak to him.

He looked down. He still held it open. The words were a blur, as if the light was suddenly too dim to read by after looking at Ms. Jane Tully.

Bridget came over to take her order. She was such a sharp contrast to Ms. Jane Tully that it was almost as if they weren't the same species. Bridget was taller than the average woman—Jane was taller still. The waitress was generously built in all the right places, fit without being either slim or heavy—Jane was sleek as a fighter jet. And Jane's immaculate blonde waterfall outshone Bridget's pleasantly tangled brunette.

"Something strong."

"We have some Guinness, love. Would that do for ya?"

Aaron often wondered if Bridget camped up her Yorkshire accent for the tourists—a long way north of this central Gloucestershire pub. If so, he'd never caught her out on it, so it was hard to tell. Like her age. She was either eighteen but looked twenty-five, or she was living proof that fifty was the new thirty. It seemed to switch from one moment to the next. At present—in fluorescent green sneakers and aiming her bright smile like a weapon—she was somewhere in between, making sport of gently teasing Americans.

"Yes," Jane's tone stayed flat. "A Guinness is fine."

"Would ya be wanting a pint or a half?" Bridget was enjoying this far too much.

It was the first time he'd seen any uncertainty in the newcomer. She glanced at the waitress and then briefly toward him. He let go of an edge of the paper to reach for his own glass.

Before he could raise it and say, "This is a pint. You probably are after a half," the center section of the newspaper fluttered away and scattered on the floor. He set his glass down quickly, grabbed for the falling section and missed, then banged his elbow on an unforgiving knob of stone sticking out of the old wall.

Jerking upright, he knocked the table and almost lost his pint to the floor.

At Snoop's bark he rapped his elbow hard again.

Jane's still, blue eyes simply watched him dissolve into a state of total ineptitude.

"I'll have the size glass he's having," she gave no reaction to the sad state of affairs that was Aaron Mason. Her voice had just the softest gracing of Southern, probably from one of the Carolinas, only added to her air of perfect sophistication. Finally Jane unleashed a *hint* of a smile, which focused all his attention on her lips. Good, full lips without any lipstick, but that hint was the first bit of emotion he'd seen from her. Humor beneath the chill exterior was almost a shock.

Bridget looked at him as if he'd lost his mind while he continued to fumble about—which wouldn't surprise anyone, neither his family nor his old Army unit. "Well, for a beer, you've got to go up to the bar, love. I'll just leave you a menu."

When Bridget was gone, Jane turned to him. A slight furrow of brow was all she showed.

"The alcohol and the bill at the end are handled by the barman," he filled in for her. "In England, the waitress typically offers food and attitude in equal portions—Bridget being masterful at both. I'm impressed, actually. She let me cool my heels for almost fifteen minutes first time I was in. She must like you."

Jane's look before she rose smoothly and headed for the bar said that it had nothing to do with her and everything to do with him. Wouldn't surprise him a bit.

The view from behind was just as pleasant as the one from the front. He watched her all through the long process of Hal the barman drawing a pint of Guinness and couldn't find a thing to complain about. She wore fine, but not senseless shoes —just enough heel to shape her calf nicely without getting all painfully fashionista or awkward. The dress accented without revealing. He wouldn't mind if she stayed in town for a while. Not one bit.

As she collected her glass and turned back for the table, he did his best to be looking elsewhere when she returned. Only at the last moment did he remember he was holding a newspaper and he stared down at it. It took a moment to understand that it was upside down. He didn't change it, hoping she wouldn't notice. Instead, he folded it in half and set it aside as a lost cause—almost taking out his beer glass again.

Once seated she didn't sip her beer, she quaffed down at least a quarter of it as if she was either painfully dry or wanted to get painfully drunk.

"You're so busted, by the way," again she spoke without turning from the fire.

"I am? For what?"

"There's a mirror behind the bar."

He glanced up just as Bridget moved to where Jane had been standing. Yep, his staring had been in Jane's full view the whole time.

"Shit!"

JANE LIKED that Mr. Not-at-all-smooth didn't try to deny it. Somehow that earned him more credit than any bravado or lame apology.

"Maybe if you weren't so stare-worthy in that dress."

She glanced down and felt ill. She'd forgotten about the dress.

"Were you up at the manor for that posh wedding?"

Jane *really* didn't want to be reminded of her sister's wedding. Debbie had married the Earl of Evenston's fourth son, who'd made a moderate fortune in computers. The groom hadn't been some cool, geeky programmer with a brilliant idea. Geoffrey was an arrogant prick who'd bought out a company at just the right time, bilking the early investors of their hard-won payoff because some idiot in a pub had let him know that they were just months from a ground-breaking delivery that even the board hadn't known about yet.

It had always been a life's goal for Debbie to marry into money. The shock was that she'd actually pulled it off. With anyone else, Jane would give the marriage a year at best. But Debbie was just selfish and greedy enough that they'd probably settle in nicely at the manor together over screaming fights, fine martinis, and wild affairs that would end up on the front page of the paper Mr. Unsmooth had been reading upside down.

"Can't a girl get drunk in peace here?" She turned on him and it came out far harder than she liked. *Absolute bitch.* She'd just earned the label fair and square, which made her far too much like her sister. Back to staring blankly at the fire, "Sorry."

"Bad day?"

"Understatement of the bloody century."

"Century's still young yet. Besides, you'll want to be careful with that," his warning tone made her look over at him. "The B-word over here is worse than our F-word back home. *Ruddy* will get the spirit of it without offending the masses."

"Don't need a *bloody* linguistics lesson today either," she went to turn away but his laugh stopped her. "What?"

"To think that I worry about English waitresses giving me attitude."

"Do you deserve it?"

He tipped his head to the side before nodding, "Maybe. Probably." Again points for honesty.

She hadn't really focused on him. He was just another thing wrong with her day. He looked like a common workman. His hair had needed a trim a few months ago. Dressed in dusty slacks, battered work boots, and a denim shirt—a denim shirt that he filled out very nicely. He obviously worked hard with his hands, they were as powerfully muscled as the forearms sticking out past his rolled-up sleeves.

Geoffrey's hand, when she'd shaken it and then wished for a restroom to wash off the feeling, had never lifted anything heavier than a fountain pen. How could Debbie want to be touched by those hands? Debbie wouldn't care. She'd be thinking about the massive checks Geoffrey could sign with that fountain pen to accommodate her slightest whim. He'd given her a hot pink Ferrari as a wedding gift this morning. Jane couldn't wait for Debbie to explain she couldn't drive a manual. Maybe Geoffrey couldn't either. Wouldn't that be the perfect joke?

Mr. Unsmooth was handsome in a hard way. Not all square-jawed or chisel-featured. It was his eyes, she decided. He'd seen things with those dark eyes, uncomfortable things. Things people like her probably didn't want to know about.

Now it was her turn to laugh.

"What?"

She shook her head and knocked back more of her beer. It felt so good, smooth and cool with just the slightest cleansing of carbonation. Smooth, mule-kick beer. She should have the bartender set up a whole line of them.

"Come on. You owe me," his voice was almost as deep as his eyes. The kind of voice a woman could wrap around her on a cold night.

"For what?"

"For revealing how much of a dolt I can be around a beautiful woman."

Maybe the beer was having a fast effect on her empty stomach —or maybe it was the two large glasses of wine and no food she'd had before leaving the wedding—but she couldn't find a fault in his argument.

"Spill it," he made it sound like an order but he had a good smile and she let it sway her.

"My sister's wedding is only half over. I should take you back for the second half to meet the groom, Geoffrey. I'm sure the two of you could be such pals."

He almost spat his beer out on her in shock. "Your sister is marrying Geoffrey, the Third Worm of Evenston?"

"Fourth Worm." What an apt description.

"No, I hear that the eldest brother is a good bloke. It's the younger three that are horrors, especially Geoffrey."

"Horrors?" Maybe she should warn her sister, not that Debbie would ever listen to her. But her mother had made her promise to take care of Debbie. It's the only reason she'd come to the wedding in the first place. There was still a chance that—

"No, not the way I can see you're thinking. Just egomaniac twits."

"Peas in a pod."

He looked at her strangely. No surprise really. Nothing Debbie ever did could surprise her. Disappoint? Always. Surprise? Not anymore.

Jane drank more of her beer, confused to discover that she was into the dregs. How had that happened so fast?

His beer was still nearly full.

"Well, are you going to finish that up?"

He inspected his barely-touched beer, "Why, are you wanting it?"

"No," she did her best to make the yeasty burp ladylike and felt that she succeeded admirably. "I'm just thinking that you'll want to finish that before you go to meet Geoffrey. There are some things that should not be done sober."

CHAPTER 2

Thankfully Hal the barman was a bit of a dandy—at least by Cotswold standards. He always kept his graying hair perfectly combed and always wore a tie. Aaron tried to remember if he'd ever seen him wear the same tie twice, but couldn't bring a repeat to mind. Hal had a spare one tucked away in the back in case of spills. It was one of his milder ones—plain, fire-engine red compared to the burgundy red, covered with the gold lions of Cambridge University he was wearing himself.

Aaron had vetoed the idea of running up to his small room close under the eaves on the third floor to change. One, he didn't have any clothes better than these. Two, he didn't want to risk Jane Tully getting away. And three, it might give him time to wonder what the hell he was doing, but that hadn't troubled him much lately. Whatever came next was fine. Whatever.

After Aaron's third failed attempt to knot the tie, Jane took over. It placed them toe-to-toe in front of the bar with her hands at his throat. Her breath smelled vaguely of Guinness, but she herself smelled of wildflowers. If it was a perfume, it was perfectly understated. It if was her, it was absolutely luscious. Her motions were smooth and precise despite pounding down the pint. He'd

13

bet she would be that same way when well plowed under. It seemed she was about halfway to potted already. He figured that the gentlemanly thing to do was to go along for the ride to make sure she didn't get herself into trouble. That was his excuse for going with her and he was sticking to it.

Then she slipped the finished knot much too tightly around his throat and he hoped that he merely survived the evening. He eased it out and then noticed a small black horse stitched into a yellow background in the center of the tie.

He looked up at Hal.

"If a sorry sod like you," Hal aimed a blunt finger at the center of Aaron's chest, "is going up to the manor for that posh affair, you better do something to pretend you have a bit of class now, hadn't you?"

"But Hal, why do *you* have a Ferrari tie?"

Hal laid a finger beside his nose. "You never know, mate. You never know." Then he offered a broad wink and turned back to the next pint he had to draw.

Jane was tugging at his arm and he had no choice but to follow along.

After the first few steps, Aaron wrenched his hip around and informed his bad leg that they would not be limping tonight. He'd be damned if he was going to look any more broken in front of Jane Tully than he already was.

She stepped out of the pub and turned the wrong way for the manor house. The sun was bright and he had to stop and blink hard to adapt his eyesight. After the noise of the crowded pub, the village was impossibly sedate. The sun would be setting soon and there was a freshness to the warm spring air. The busy truck traffic and the day tourists had petered out for the evening and Fosse-on-the-Wold was small enough that the locals simply walked to get anywhere.

She didn't complain when he turned her about and they passed the pub going in the other direction.

His attempts to draw her out were lost in nerves—her nerves. She suddenly turned into Miss Flighty Female Window Shopper, wanting to stop and look in every window. Before he quite lost all respect for her, she stopped abruptly and spoke in a completely different voice.

"Oh, that *is* pretty."

He glanced into the window of the hardware store. She was looking at a roll of floral wallpaper. Not his thing, but it was well done. Pale colors, elegant design.

Aaron figured out that she had no interest in any of what she was cooing at and had been deploying delay tactics. He broke her free before she turned both their stomachs and headed down Sheep Street—an alleyway so narrow between towering stone walls that they had to walk single file. It had been used when Fosse was still a major wool market. The sheep had been run into the town square on market day and the lane was narrow enough that the sheep, too, had to go single file and could be easily counted.

Regrettably, by following the footpath that led out the end of Sheep Street and through a small wood, they approached the back of the manor rather quickly.

"Are you sure this is the way? I didn't come this way." Even half-soused, she was steady on her feet, walking with fast, deter-mined strides until they reached the two tall hedgerows that met above them in a green-arched canopy. She slowed way down and looked at it in wonder. "It's like a fairy tale."

"You must have come round by the drive and the road. Much longer that way." And he wished he'd thought to take her back the same way to have more time with her. Perhaps sober her up a bit as well.

"Birds," she said, looking upward into the branches and only staying upright by her strong hold on his elbow. Crows and turtledoves and sparrows and wrens and who knew what all were making their standard cacophony whenever someone walked too close to their hedgerow nests.

"Birds," he agreed and led her on. A pheasant strode across the path with a carefully considered grandeur.

Jane watched it wide-eyed but offered no comment until it was well gone. "Bird," she whispered again.

"Bird," he concurred. Their slow pace was giving Aaron time to have second thoughts. "I haven't crashed a wedding since third year of high school."

She started walking again, as if trying to move with the pheasant's studied nonchalance. She did an exquisite job of it.

He wished he could figure out how to stare and walk beside her simultaneously.

"You've crashed a wedding before? Debbie always did things like that. I was the good daughter."

He'd bet she was. He'd also bet that well-started-on-the-way-to-drunk wasn't normal for her either. She was handling it with a certain *Alice in Wonderland* quality of how new and odd everything was.

The sunlight was dappling over her hair as they came out of the hedgerow tunnel: warm gold in shadow, brilliant in direct sunlight. What the shadows of the pub had suggested, the late afternoon light revealed. Her features weren't merely fine, he'd call them patrician—highborn from fine stock. She walked through the woods in a dress that probably cost more than all of his clothes together, and maybe his car back in the States as well. An elegant nymph or Faerie Queen. Basically, way the hell out of his league.

"Tell me about the wedding you crashed."

"Uh..." *Right! Think about something else than her warm voice and the way her hand on his arm felt.* "Me and a mate. Seventeen. Looking for any way to get free beer. He got the beer. I ended up making off with the prettiest bridesmaid instead."

"Were you good to her?"

"And her to me." They'd dated for all of senior year. Mary had gone to Vassar and he'd gone to Iraq with the US Army. Even the breakup had been easy—they both knew it wouldn't have lasted. At least that's what Mary had said and he'd believed her; she'd always been smarter about that sort of thing.

"Why do you talk a bit as if you're from England, but your accent says Vermont?"

That was something he didn't want to answer. "I've been in England a while," which covered almost none of the reason. "Because I can never again be who I was. So, I'm desperately pretending to be someone different." Now *there* was an uncomfortable truth.

They arrived at the wedding from the back field of the estate, cutting off any response she might have made.

The Evenston estate had been, unimaginatively, Banks Manor when it belonged to a banker. Mr. Banker had been caught embezzling from his hedge fund. The manor had sold at fire-sale prices ten years earlier because the recession that had swept through Europe had affected the very wealthy as well as the common man. But not the earl—a cautious man, he'd invested carefully and snapped up the twenty-six-bedroom manor and seven hundred acres around as his new primary residence, restoring its name to simply Fosse-on-the-Wold Manor. He had set aside the sprawling northern dairy estate—bequeathed to his family by a grateful Queen Elizabeth I for services in battle—to his eldest son.

Aaron felt that Fosse was a sensible choice for the earl's second home as the town was already thick with tributes to the sixteenth-century queen, from the name of the pub to the portraits worked into the stained glass windows of St. Stephen's Church.

He could spot no sign of the recent transition—everything looked as if the earl had been in residence here down a centuries-long lineage. To the west lay rolling fields filled with sheep and lambs. To the north was a broad field divided into neat half-acre pens. Each pen held a beautiful racing horse. They pranced along the other side of the immaculate white fence as he and Jane passed by.

"Ooo. You're so pretty," Jane spoke to the horses.

Aaron's attention was fixed to the south, toward the wedding gathering. He did a rapid risk assessment—not *all* of his skills had been lost. A hundred and twenty...three people, with perhaps ten percent more inside based on the current dynamics of the situation, milled about on the vast back lawn. Eleven children, under the careful control of two harried nannies. Tables set out under white umbrellas. A croquet court. A vast table of food, watched over by two carved-ice pheasants each the size of a small elephant.

Jane was among the upper third here for the cost of her dress, but only barely. The worst dressed of this lot still wouldn't be found in any department store. Money seemed to drip off many of the women.

The center of power was obvious even at a glance. A very proper-looking older man must be the Earl of Evenston. Men and women stood with him in a rough circle, but they all left a slightly greater space around the one man. None of them had military training, a part of him he'd thought long dead noted. It would be a trivial task for a sniper to pick him out as the leader. *This is a wedding, not a battlefield,* Aaron reminded himself. At least he hoped not.

That's when he picked out the bride—obvious in her stand-out designer gown. Lavender, so clearly not the wedding gown, merely the post-wedding, pre-whatever-was-next-on-the-agenda, showing-off-her-newfound-wealth gown.

"Bet that cost more than a bob or two."

"Seven thousand British pounds."

He couldn't quite read envy or disgust in Jane's voice. But definitely worth more than his car—even fifty thousand miles earlier when he'd bought it from the used lot over in Rutland. Hal hadn't been kidding about him being completely out of his class, and a red Ferrari tie wasn't going to make the least bit of difference. *Time to gear up, soldier.*

The key players were all in the earl's inner circle. His four sons and their own women were in play as well—the third son literally, as he had his hand on the ass of one of the bridesmaids while his wife stood on his other side. The gesture would only be visible to someone arriving through the woods. The bridesmaid was leaning in, not away.

"You," he turned to Jane, "are not to leave my side. If you need to go to the toilet, I'll escort you to the door and wait for you. Are we clear on that?" He was not going to have the First or Second Worm of Evenston putting his hands anywhere on the tipsy Jane.

"Yes, sir," she shot him a mock salute—that he almost returned.

"I'm not a sir, I work for a living," the standard Army enlisted reply slipped out before he could stop it. So much gone. Now he really did work for a living. Manual labor. How the mighty had fallen.

Well, he warned himself, *it is time to dig deep, soldier.* His right hip was hurting from his efforts to hide his limp. He wasn't going to be able to sustain that all night without some painkillers. His unfinished beer would have been enough to offset a workday, except it was still back at the pub. But this would take something more; it had been a while since he'd worked to hide that damning limp.

Time to confront the beast. He led Jane toward the heart of the enemy.

"We'll be stuck until the cake cutting," Jane whispered breathily in his ear. "It won't be for a while. We can still run away, maybe to Italy." He liked the sound of that.

"We're on a mission, then. Operation Cake—a surgical strike, then bug out."

"Operation Sugar."

"Yes, ma'am. Whatever you say, ma'am."

She squeezed his arm like a laugh.

Then she clenched it hard enough he almost yelped. Her nails were short, but his shirt was thin and her grip strong.

~

"THERE YOU ARE, sis. You know that I've had the servants looking just everywhere for you," Debbie whisked across the lawn like the Wicked Witch of the West. The belled skirt made it look as if she slid rather than walked. Jane glanced at the perfect lawn but couldn't spot the inevitable trail of slime her sister left wherever she went.

"Fat chance," Jane cursed herself for going straight to nasty but Debbie brought out the worst in her.

Debbie had never cared crap about where Jane was. Though now that she had servants to order about, maybe she had sent them looking for her sister, just so that she could issue commands.

Besides, Debbie wasn't paying any attention to her. Instead she was looking at…

At…

Jane turned to look at…*him*. Hadn't she asked his name? She must have. She'd invited the man to her sister's high society wedding so he must have a name. This *so* wasn't like her.

Unsure of what to do next, she turned to Debbie to explain… something. Except Debbie was still looking at…*him*. With a look Jane knew all too well.

Jane grabbed tighter onto *his* arm. How many boyfriends had Debbie ripped away from her with her deep-red hair, her pumped-up breasts, and her low-cut dresses? Mom never really saw. The Debbie she'd always described was frail, uncertain, and in desperate need of protection from the cruel world. The Debbie that Jane knew was a spoiled, cast-iron bitch who would have sold their mother to the devil for the price of a new pair of Jimmy Choo pumps. Jane tried to count how many boyfriends and potential boyfriends Debbie had stolen and felt a twirl of vertigo at how fast the number climbed.

"Hi," *his* voice had dropped about half an octave lower than it had already been. Very dangerous. Very alpha-male sexy.

Jane had never dated alpha-male sexy—not her type. She had tended toward intelligent, often professors. *Had!* She'd never make that mistake again. Squinting at the various men who were turning to watch the fun, none of them were even half as alpha-male sexy as her nameless escort. Maybe she should give him a try.

But it was too late.

He held out his right hand to Debbie. Jane's hand about his right elbow also moved forward. She started to remove it because that was just too silly. Then he reached across with his left hand and clamped her hand into place as he shook Debbie's. His grip keeping her in place wasn't merely strong; it was powerful.

"I'm Aaron Mason. Thank you for having me."

Aaron. Aaron. Aaron. Jane repeated it in her head a few more times to be sure that she had it down. *Mason. Aaron Mason.*

"My pleasure," Debbie drawled out in her best I-don't-care-if-it's-my-wedding-day-come-fuck-me-in-the-hydrangeas voice.

Jane braced herself for it. Waited for the gut slam of yet another man being caught by purchased breasts and her coy moue practiced in the mirror since birth.

Aaron extracted his hand from Debbie's, but didn't let go of his left hand clamping Jane's to his right elbow. Possessively. As if he actually meant to stay beside her.

Debbie's eyes narrowed, reading the same signals, which meant Jane wasn't merely imagining them.

Her sister's look said this wasn't over yet, but the committee-to-repulse-boarders moved in and trumped Debbie's next move.

"Debra, darling." The groom began his approach. Debbie had always hated being called Debra, but she hadn't trained the Third Worm of Evenston yet. He was accompanied by one of the bridesmaids, who was obviously hoping to count coup on the nuptial night, and another of the worm sons. They came across the perfect green lawn like a flock of descending vultures to rend her and Aaron's (*Aaron's*) flesh. The earl and the eldest son, Jane noted, hung back, doing their best to be polite about the whole thing.

"Am I going to get you in trouble?" She kept her voice down to a whisper. Aaron (*Aaron, Aaron*) worked in this town and these were powerful men.

"The best defense is a good attack," he patted her hand without releasing it and turned to face the onslaught.

~

AARON AVOIDED the fight by trumping their move. Moments before the unwelcoming committee reached his position, he stepped aside, almost losing Jane to the manicured lawn. He'd forgotten that she wouldn't be trained to read his body language like a Special Operations soldier could—*remember to give clearer signals.*

Another step sideways—foreshadowed by a firm tug with his elbow—placed a waiter with a tray of champagne glasses neatly between the two of them and the incoming squad. He took two flutes, trusting Jane's degree of panic to keep her holding on to his arm after he released his hold on her. She did. Good.

Following the flow of the waiter, a seemingly casual stroll at a forty-five degree angle of attack, set up a tortoise topiary as a running block. Looping behind an incoming lad with a tray of finger canapes, he came up beside the earl and his Number One son. He calculated that they were his best shot at sanctuary.

Tactics 101. Come at them head-on, then you're the enemy. Come up beside them, they'll wait to see if you're a friend.

"This is really a splendid house, sir. I was so glad when Jane offered me the opportunity to see it up close." Aaron launched in as if they were already in mid-conversation and he and Jane went way back. *Old friend of the family, mate. Don't mind me.* He waved his full champagne glass at the towering edifice of the manor house, while Jane focused (a little too deliberately) on emptying her own glass. Next time he'd have to find coffee.

Before the earl could do more than start a bewildered acknowledgement, he continued.

"I know that the foundation is Jacobean. It's a pity that none of that survived the fire of 1232, except that base run."

Jackpot. He could see that the earl didn't know that fact about his own home.

"Fire turns the Cotswolds' yellow limestone reddish when it is exposed to high heat. That's why the lowest part of the outer wall is red. I love the Byzantine design of the main house and the blending of the two wing additions: the Gothic of 1497 and the early Baroque of 1651 to repair the damage from your Civil War. It wouldn't have worked if not for the consistent use of the Birdlip Limestone Formation." For perhaps the first time since he'd started working English stone, he blessed Trent's wandering stories. The old mason who he had apprenticed himself to was so dug in to the history of the town, stone by stone, that he never seemed to run out of tales to tell. And many of those were about the construction of "that monstrosity on the hill."

Monstrosity or not, Aaron blessed Trent now. Soon he and Jane were away from the initial hazards of the wedding party and firmly entrenched behind enemy lines. They were escorted on a personal tour of the interior—only the earl and his first son along for the ride. Large scales of capital had been used to purchase ancestral quality antiques to fill the rooms. Thankfully the twenty-first century interior designer had been expensive enough to have more taste than the ancient architectural ones.

As long as they were talking about stone, Aaron could at least pretend he knew what he was doing. A long-ago part of his training had been in interrogation techniques. The "Knowledge-able Friend" technique was an undercover tactic run from a few facts and then asking apparently casual questions to keep the targets talking. Normally he'd be looking for the element of operational opportunity.

This evening he was only after survival.

Survival, and not letting Jane anywhere near her poisonous sister.

～

"HOW DID YOU DO IT?"

"What?" Aaron (*Aaron*) responded with all innocence.

Jane sat shoulder-to-shoulder with him on the old limestone wall around the front of the stables. This wall, instead of having the normal vertically-set capstones that Aaron (*Aaron*) said kept the sheep from jumping over, had a rounded cap of smooth mortar more suited to sitting on.

No one was likely to find them here. Night had fallen, and while the bright Chinese lanterns (which had been kitschy even for Debbie) lit the grounds far and wide, the only thing here was moonlight and stars shining down on the broad Cotswold valley. The fine racing horses were bedded down in the majestic stone building behind them and the rolling valley before them offered pale fields crisscrossed by dark lines of hedgerows and stone walls. A distant field of yellow rapeseed (that Aaron had said was the same as canola) shone in the moonlight like a magic carpet.

"Well, I slipped the waiter a ten pound note if he promised to deliver two slices of cake without exposing our secret operation." He tapped the edge of the dinner plate in his lap. She looked down at the plate, which held two enormous pieces of cake, but couldn't remember who they had operated on to get them.

"Which secret operation?" Maybe it was a secret from her too.

"Operation Sugar."

"Oh, right." She'd forgotten but she knew about *that* secret operation. Or was there some other one that she didn't know

24

about? Not knowing if the vague swirls in the moonlit canola fields were due to a breeze or the fact that the world had slipped off its axis, she decided to keep her focus on Aaron.

The last hours had been a dizzying whirl of architecture, family history, brandy in the library (Earl Conrad Evenston had also appeared glad of an excuse to temporarily escape the wedding), champagne for the toasts, more champagne for Debbie's long-winded dinner speech that had clearly and carefully included their deceased parents but left out her only sister. That last had bothered several in the crowd, though Jane couldn't care at all. She tried a what-do-I-care dismissive hand wave, but it felt silly.

Besides, she'd had enough to drink that Debbie could break into a striptease on the wedding table and Jane wouldn't bat an eye. Again, wouldn't be surprised.

Aaron's whispered, "She's even more of a bitch than I first thought," had been all the support she needed.

Somehow Aaron's presence had given her permission to let loose on the stranglehold she'd been using to stay under control. Of course, she'd let loose in other ways as well. The last time she'd been this drunk…college…maybe?

No, the final night of Larry Jenkins. Her final academic lover— ever! Now that she'd spent a night on the arm of an alpha-sexy male, she was never going back. He'd been so protective of her and instead of being irritating, it had been charming. *Got some news, Mom. Debbie isn't the one who needs protecting.* Not that Jane did either, but it was nice to try it on for one night, like a cashmere ensemble. It definitely didn't suck.

Jane remembered that last night of Larry. Her Last-Larry. Of Larry the Lech. Of… She had been riding high from finishing an overnight systems upgrade hours ahead of plan, only to come home to… Old story.

Arriving home at two a.m. she'd found her almost-fiancé and some coed bimbo in pigtails passed out naked on the living room rug. They'd still been bleary enough with alcohol that she'd been able to get them both outside and lock the door before they really came to. She'd taken their half-finished bottle of whiskey and killed it off herself with her back against the front door while they pounded on the other side. Something about wanting their clothes, but she couldn't rouse herself enough to care.

She *had* finally given the clothes to the nice policeman who some neighbor had called to take the two "disturbers of the peace" away—after she'd made sure to recover the house key from Larry's pants pocket. *Good old Jane Tully was efficient if nothing else,* she'd assured herself. She'd also sorted through Ms. Bimbo's purse (turned out she was a Bimbette). Jane had made sure the policeman noticed the birthday on the ID. Barely old enough to drive a car (*not* old enough to be in one of Larry's college classes). Once the courts were done with him, apparently Ms. Bimbette hadn't been the first in line, it had turned out that Larry wasn't going to be a problem for a long time.

Now, instead of weaving, as the floor had done that night, the old limestone wall seemed to be floating on a gentle sea.

Of course, she wouldn't even be here in England if her career hadn't—

She didn't want to think about that.

"Tell me something. Anything!" Jane desperately needed a distraction from the morass of her thoughts.

"I screwed up our operation."

"No you didn't. You were magnilliquent. Manifiquent. Magnificent," she finally wrapped her tongue around it. He'd protected her at every turn—her staunch, dusty champion in the red racing tie. Maybe it was a magic tie, because none of it should have worked, but on Aaron it had. They'd survived.

"I forgot to tell the waiter to bring forks along with the cake."

Jane looked down at the plate that seemed to glow in the moonlight. The two massive slices of cake nearly filled it to the gold-trimmed rim—real gold, she'd wager—but there were no forks to be seen.

Today was so thoroughly not the day she'd been expecting. The horrors of her sister throughout the preparation and ceremony, the unexpectedness of finding a White Knight with a Vermont accent in the dim corner of an English pub, Debbie's multiple forays at Aaron throughout the endless evening (and her utter failure at taking him away from Jane—major happy dance), and the copious amounts of alcohol.

She herself wasn't what she was expecting either. With each passing hour, Jane had shed another piece of Debbie's ability to affect her mood until she was practically giddy.

"That's not me at all."

"What isn't?"

"Practically giddy. I'm big on the practical part. Always had that down. Giddy? That's like new territory." She always hated it when people used "like" that way. Thankfully she was too drunk to hate herself at the moment.

Aaron nodded in the moonlight as if she was making perfect sense. Or as if he already knew that giddy wasn't really her, but more like, dunno, someone else.

She broke off a big bite of the cake with her fingers and bit down on it. Frosting caught on her fingers and lips.

"Yum," she managed around the mouthful. "Dark chocolate with cherry jam and cream cheese frosting. My sister always hires the best caterers when someone else is paying."

Aaron broke off a small piece and snapped it down neatly between clean white teeth that shone in the night. "It's good."

"You can't tell from that little bit." She broke off a huge piece and aimed it at him. When he opened his mouth to protest, she shoved it in. Icing smeared his nose, cheeks, and chin as she struggled to correct her aim. She finally managed to land it properly.

Aaron managed a "Mmgrumph" as he attempted to wrestle it down without losing half of it down his front.

"Don't mess up Hal's tie," she wiped at the white frosting dotting his nose and chin and then licked it off her fingers. It took several tries to get it all.

"I'm trying to be good here," Aaron's voice was deep and dangerous once he could speak again.

"Why? About what?"

He merely snarled and looked away.

"You're so…" she didn't have the right word for it, "…male."

"Meaning what?"

What did she mean? He was her White Knight. Staunch and artful. By siding with the Earl of Evenston and his first son whose name had escaped her again—though she still remembered Aaron (*Aaron*)—none of the others had dared to mess with them. Even Debbie had finally backed off after one particularly pithy look from her new father-in-law. Her new husband might be wealthy, but one glance at the manor house said where the real money and the power of this family resided.

Aaron's looks had grown on Jane during the long evening. Through her near permanent attachment to his elbow, she'd felt not only his muscles, but his mood until she could tell when he was hesitant (rarely) or decisive (pretty much all the time), ready to move (he seemed permanently poised for action) or momentarily relaxed (almost never). She slipped her hand about his arm again and wondered at the strange tension that had been there, especially for the latter half of the evening.

He was trying to be good, huh? Well, she was pretty *bloody* sick of being good. Being bad sounded like a *good* thing right at the moment.

She searched around for the champagne glass she'd brought with her but couldn't spot it. Aaron had one propped on the wall to his other side. No, he had two. How had her glass gotten way over there?

Leaning across to reach for it, Jane could feel the warmth of him in the cool night.

When her chest brushed his, he cursed softly, "Bloody hell."

"Careful with that. The B-word over here—"

Suddenly those strong arms of his were wrapped around her, pulling her body hard against his. There wasn't a thing tentative about his kiss, rich with chocolate, cherry, and cream cheese.

If her seat on the wall had been floating before, it was suddenly a rocket ride upward. England, the Cotswolds, the wedding, all fell away until there was only the heat of his kiss crushing against her lips.

Someone moaned. Jane was fairly sure it was her. No one had ever kissed her that way: so powerful, so self-assured, so full of need—for her!

One moment she was in the best kiss that had ever happened to womankind and the next she was sitting alone on the wall watching the back of a man as he strode away.

He didn't go past ten paces.

But they were hard, pounding strides that seemed to punch his anger into the ground.

He jolted to a halt with a sharp hiss of anger that seemed to shatter the night.

She took his glass of champagne and slammed it back.

Spotting hers in her other hand, she emptied that one as well.

Rejection. She was not ready to deal with one more moment of that.

Aaron should just leave. He should just walk away.

But his hip had finally given up on hiding his limp and he couldn't stop the hiss of pain. The pain and the stupidity. He'd kissed her. The beautiful, drunk, and obviously hurt woman that he'd committed to protect—he'd failed to protect her from *him*.

The guys in his US Army unit had always teased him about

being so square about women. But during his tenure with the British SAS, he'd fit right in.

Sure, there were always blokes who treated women as if they all were fast and easy. But most of the Brits were soldiers who knew what was proper.

"Proper" did *not* include kissing a drunk woman simply because she was being vulnerable. Nor running his hand down the side of her perfect breast, past her waist, and onto the delicious swell of her hip. Her chiffon and lace dress hid none of her heat or softness. And proper definitely didn't include how close he'd just come to pulling down the long, side zipper and tossing her naked onto the grass.

He watched the stars—Vega was up, Cygnus the Swan was rising—until he had himself together. At least somewhat together. Then he turned to face her. He'd apologize, even if he wouldn't mean it. Women like Jane weren't for broken men like him, but he didn't want her one bit less for all of that.

She had lain down atop the wall, every perfect curve accented by her dress shimmering in the moonlight, shifting and reflecting the light with each breath—the Faerie Queen indeed. A horse sighed in its sleep as it shifted in the nearby stables. A thin trail of music sounded from the wedding, sounding as if it was coming from miles away.

He knew he was hopelessly befuddled. Not drunk. He hadn't dared risk that, needing his wits in that crowd. But Jane Tully made him think serious thoughts. The kind of thoughts that weren't his to think.

"Well, you can't leave her on the bloody wall all night."

"Careful with that B-word..." her voice was a whisper on the night that trailed off into the darkness. Her eyes remained closed.

He staggered back to the wall, limping hard now that his hip had given up.

"Can't sleep here, my queen. Where are you staying? I'll walk you there." *I'll limp you there and hope that you're too drunk and it's too dark to notice.*

She waved a hand vaguely toward the manor house, then tucked it back under her cheek.

"Bloody hell," he whistled out softly.

She didn't respond this time.

He couldn't return her to that den of vipers, especially not drunk on a wedding night.

"Come along, Queen Jane," he took her hand and tugged her to her feet.

Instead of taking his arm, she slid up against his side with her arm around his waist. She fit like—

Don't go there, lad.

His attempts to disengage her failed, so he finally slid his arm around her waist and led her back up the path through the woods.

He'd managed to avoid the dancing earlier, partly because of his aching hip and partly because he didn't dare the risk of holding her close.

Now they walked as close as lovers, moving slowly and, courtesy of his sore hip and bad knee, arrhythmically along the moonlit path.

CHAPTER 3

Jane woke, then wished she hadn't. Her head throbbed, aching like it had been overrun by an entire phalanx of wedding guests.

Wedding!

No wonder she felt ill.

She unburied her face enough from the pillow to inspect her environs. The first thing she spotted was a bottle of aspirin and a glass of water on the rustic night table. She took two and considered a third. Maybe later.

Bless the holy ghost of foresight that had her put it there.

Then she looked a little farther afield and saw her dress hanging from a hook on the back of the door. Except the door didn't have delicate wood-carved panels. It looked like a battered old wooden door—stout, but from another century. The room was low-ceilinged and part of it sloped even lower. Two small gable windows let in the first light of dawn.

There was only enough space for the bed and two chairs. If this was the manor house, she'd ended up in entirely the wrong room, though she liked it better. It was small and cozy. Comfortable. The room they'd given her in the manor house, as the bride's sister and only remaining family member, had been vast and austere.

Closing her eyes for the worst of it, she managed to push herself upright. The room spun, even with her eyes closed. Hungover or still drunk? She couldn't tell, but either way it was awful.

She hadn't even taken off her bra and panties, though she'd tugged on a long t-shirt. A t-shirt that…she didn't recognize. It had the blazing red B on a field of blue for the Boston Red Sox, instead of the stylish A of the vastly superior Atlanta Braves. Some damned Yankee had trash-dressed her while she'd been under the influence.

It did smell deliciously male though. Just like…

Then she focused on the narrow space by the foot of the bed.

Aaron! (*Aaron Aaron*) some ridiculous part of her brain echoed though she wasn't sure why. He was stretched out on the floor with a pair of rolled-up pants for a pillow and a jacket pulled over him for a blanket.

And she was in his bed wearing bra and panties and a t-shirt she didn't remember putting on.

"Jane, you ignorant slut." The old *Saturday Night Live* line didn't feel any better than the first time she'd heard it. Debbie had discovered it online, of course, and used it at every opportunity since. Jane was surprised her sister hadn't worked it into last night's toast. No, because then she would have had to say Jane's name. Having her sister proven right about the ignorant slut part wasn't helping matters.

Jane remembered a kiss. At least she was fairly sure that she did. A kiss of cherry and dark chocolate. There had definitely been moonlight involved, or at least in her fantasy there had been.

And a second kiss. One that had more flesh taking part in it. A kiss in between a low voice coaxing her out of her dress, which she suspected hadn't been hard, and into this t-shirt, which she vaguely recalled protesting. She'd bet good money that her protests last night had nothing to do with team affiliations.

What was the protocol in this situation? Aaron Mason had…

Jane, you ignorant—

She opted for the chicken's way out.

Ducking out into the hall, she changed from t-shirt to dress at the top of a narrow, extremely steep stairwell that threatened to pitch her overboard at every breath. She dumped the Boston Red Sox shirt against the door where he'd find it, and bolted.

Three floors down the twisting stair, she stumbled into the shadowed pub from last night where she'd first met him. Jane slipped through the closed pub and out into the dawn light. She'd have run, if she could. Her head and her stability, even on mid-heels, was having nothing to do with that. How much had she had to drink?

Too much because her memory was blurred? Or not enough because she'd woken up with the vague memory of a roaring kiss that ran heat all up her body even now?

If that sliver of a memory had survived her drunken episode, what had the kiss really been like? Too bad she'd missed it.

AARON WORKED ON THE WALL. The ancient dry-laid stone fences crisscrossed the Cotswold landscape in every direction. With no mortar to hold them, building a traditional stone wall was as much art as science. *Rebuilding* one was art, science, and a great deal of manual labor.

First, the old, tumbledown wall—torn apart by ivy in some places, by weather and shifting soil in others—had to be disassembled. It was always a surprise to him what a great mound of stone came out of a wall four feet high and eighteen inches wide. The Cotswold walls, unlike the gray fieldstone ones of his parents' Vermont farm, were made of three walls, not one. The two outer layers were of laid stone, then there was a several inch gap in the center that was filled with all the smaller limestone rubble—each piece of which was handset rather than dumped in.

He'd been working with Trent, a lifelong mason, for almost three months now and the walls still felt wrong. A Vermont wall was anchored with one- and two-man stones—named for how many men it took to lever one into place with a pry bar. A good wall was all about well-placed smaller chinking stones to keep the bigger ones in alignment. Here the stones were consistently a few inches thick, moderately flat, and rarely more than a foot square— one- or two-*handed* stones.

Trent had no use for "all that metric crap," not for wall building. Aaron had teased him for using something as modern as the English foot rather than the Roman *pes*. The old man's face was lined enough that it had been hard to tell if he smiled at that or not.

"You really are American," Trent greeted him from across the wall Aaron was working on.

"Why do you say that?"

"It's Saturday. No Englishman works on a garden wall on a Saturday unless he's some Londoner down for the weekend looking to get his hands dirty. Only an American does that when stonework has been his doings for all the rest of the week."

Aaron merely shrugged as he knelt down to scrape the bottom of the shallow trench into the right shape for the first stone. His knee and hip stung after last night's abuse, but pain was an old friend and he didn't feel the need to be sharing that with Trent.

"Nothing better to do on a Saturday."

By training he was a very light sleeper, but still Jane had slipped out without rousing him. Of course he didn't usually lie awake half the night telling himself not to climb into bed with a drunken woman.

Jane had been a vision in the unexpectedly simple, white cotton underwear that she'd worn beneath the stunning dress. A vision that had wrapped her arms around him and offered a full body kiss. He'd let himself get lost in the feel of her skin, of her body and lips pressed against him, so soft, so alive. He'd forgotten what that felt like to hold a woman so close as if to never let her go. In her moderate heels, they'd matched in height. Barefoot, she was shorter, softer, more vulnerable, and it had fed his need for her until it was almost intolerable.

A slight shiver had run through her: from being mostly naked in his cool room, the narrowness of her escape from the wedding, or some backlash from all the alcohol she'd kept finding despite his best efforts to divert the flow. He didn't know, but it had been enough to break the spell. She'd been incoherently argumentative when he pulled one of his t-shirts over her head. He'd thought to reach under and undo her bra, but didn't trust himself. It hadn't mattered, Jane had been asleep before she hit the sheets.

And he'd sat in the chair for hours watching her as the moonlight shifted across the bed through the unshuttered window.

There'd never been a woman in this room, not with him at least. Bridget had offered a time or two—though he was fairly sure that she'd just been sassing him. The longer he stayed here and watched her and the barman, the more he suspected that Hal was a very lucky man. There hadn't been a woman for Aaron since before the night in the Yemen desert that had ripped him from his one true calling and slammed him into a hospital and rehab for endless months.

And there'd never been a woman like—

"Doing a bit of dreaming there, boy." Trent sat down on a pile of the old stone and began hand-rolling one of his vile cigarettes.

Aaron selected a couple of good-sized stones for the base layer. They were particularly rough on the bottom side, so they'd grip well against the hard-packed soil.

"Heard you were up to the manor."

Small town, small news moved fast. He knew that from growing up in the five-hundred-person town of Jay, Vermont.

Fosse-on-the-Wold was no bigger. Hal, Bridget, or any of the dozen locals who'd been in the pub when they left could be the source. Aaron grunted a stone into place.

"Might have heard there was a pretty lady on your arm most of the night."

Aaron wondered at the news source for that. One of the waiters? Half the town had been called in on the preparation for the event, could have been anyone. He found a stone that he knew Trent would have used, it was a good enough fit. But Trent would never let a trainee like Aaron use because it wasn't the *perfect* stone. He tossed it aside and prowled the pile until he found the best one, half hidden by where Trent had placed his foot on it. He yanked it free and set it in place. A nice tight fit.

"Not prying into your affairs, mind."

Yeah, right.

"But it seems about time you had one, boy."

Not with a woman like Jane Tully. And not with a woman that had bolted away from him the moment she was sober enough to think straight.

A MASSIVE BIRD blew out of the brush at Jane's feet with more commotion than a rabid Atlanta Braves fan would make if the team ever made it to the World Series again.

She jerked to a halt, her eyes crossing at the pheasant—beatings its wings hard to get away from her. She hunched for a moment, half expecting the roar of a shotgun like in all those English manor movies, but the pheasant flew on unmolested.

She bent down, placing her hands on her runner's tights, and hung her head. No point in checking her pulse rate now (it would be right off the charts). She remained head down until her headache returned to merely catastrophic. The aspirin hadn't dented it and the orange juice with dry toast wasn't helping much either.

Run through the pain.

What a stupid plan, Jane Tully.

She checked her watch. Officially one of her slowest miles… ever. And that was despite running her most upbeat music list (at a very low and soothing volume).

No, wait, she'd recalibrated her phone's running app to kilometers on the flight over. That was before she found out England still used miles for distance even though almost everything else had made the transition to metric, and she hadn't reset it back to miles yet.

Kilometers were shorter, which meant it was an okay mile. No, the other way round. It was worse than her worst mile ever. She might as well be crawling for all of the progress she was making across the Cotswold countryside.

Debbie and Geoffrey were thankfully off on a Debbie-designed honeymoon and wouldn't be back for weeks from "Dear Charlie's" motor yacht currently circling Italy. Debbie had said it was eighty meters long. Two-hundred-and-sixty feet hadn't sounded likely, until her sister listed off the swimming pool, grand piano, jet skis, movie theater for twenty, servants (of course), and other amenities that every newlywed couple needed to find a happy start together.

Jane would worry about finding somewhere else to stay after she survived her run. As consolation she noted that, if she didn't survive the run, it would save her the effort of finding another place. She certainly couldn't stay at the manor, with Debbie gone and the wedding over. Especially not with the other two worm sons still in residence. That had become abundantly clear this morning over breakfast when Worm Two had tried to grope her despite their mutual hangovers. She'd felt no need to explain why he was curled up in a fetal position on the hard stone floor when a servant came in with the breakfast he'd ordered.

Jane's own wedding would be simple. A few close friends. Good food.

No champagne.

Any attempts to recall how much she'd had to drink always blurred after her arrival at the pub. Most of the evening blurred at that point.

Except for one thing.

Handsome, alpha sexy men never paid attention to her, except the ones hoping she'd be an easy lay (which she never was, not even when she tried to be). And they never ignored Debbie's come-all-ye-with-a-Y-chromosome pitch.

Yet, Aaron didn't blur. He…

And she was right back where she'd started, looping together the bits and pieces of last night that she remembered. She flexed her left hand. It was as if the entire night had been focused down to the memory of her hand tucked in the crook of his elbow. Everything else was a mash-up of varying unclarity, but she'd bet she could account for every single change in his mood through her left palm.

Except for the kiss.

That too was a blur, of a different kind.

She started up the lane once more—at least she supposed it was a lane because it was paved, but it was hard to imagine anything bigger than a MINI Cooper car fitting on it. Sheep might travel three abreast, but not four.

Right. Maybe that's why it was such a slow mile (because it couldn't be her raging hangover). It was because of all of the impossibly cute lambs, prancing about under the wild-cherry blossoms.

She was running (perhaps too strong a word for it) through a land of rolling hills, English houses of yellow stone, perfect gardens, and everywhere she turned were sheep and lambs. Black-faced, freckle-faced, and plain white sheep, each with a number spray-painted on its side in neon colors. The lambs too, some barely old enough to walk, already had numbers of their own as well. It was as if they were born with neon numbers already in place. The older lambs either chased her along the other side of the rough stone fence or scattered at her approach, all in response to some sheepy instinct she didn't understand.

Like last night when Aaron's lips had—

Damn it!

Looping again.

Glimpses of a cottage in the distance had her trotting (still too strong a word) down one lane and up another to reach it, but the cottage teased and held its distance. Most of the Cotswold houses were straightforward, square-set places. One or two stories, a slate or tile roof; they were beautiful with age and charm. Occasionally one was done in thick thatch, but they were rare. This one promised more. A fanciful window seen between two maples. A small spire that peeked over a nearby shed.

Spotting a narrow footpath that appeared to be heading in the right direction, she turned down it. Birdsong roared out of the bordering hedgerows that blocked any view to either side. It was loud enough to overpower her running playlist.

"Birds!" Last night's laughter came back to her and she turned the playlist off. Aaron beside her. His strong arm keeping her steady. His—

The hedgerow ended as abruptly as if it had been torn away.

And she was back on that same lane where the pheasant had startled her earlier. Somehow she'd come full circle, completely missing the cottage the first time. She must have been blind because it was right there.

The cottage was far cuter than anything she'd imagined. Perhaps it had been transported here while her back was turned, because she couldn't think of how else she could have missed it.

Sure you can, Jane. Head down. Playlist on. More concerned about your time and distance than—

She struggled to shut out the words but they wouldn't stop.

—than having a life.

Even Larry the fornicator had told her that when she'd seen him in court that last time. His calling her a "chilly bitch" was now permanently inscribed on the court's records. As if *she* was the cause of his seeking underage girls for sex. He was a complete sicko, but it didn't stop his words from rattling around in her head.

She had a heart. She knew it! Even if she wasn't sure where she'd left it along the way.

The cottage's stonework was obviously very old. There was a roughness to the stone, and thick green lichens growing like living paint swatches that newer work didn't have. Facts that she wouldn't have recognized before Aaron's tour of the manor house last night.

Maybe she didn't mind so much how often he was invading her thoughts, because every time they were oddly good memories.

The cottage. She'd been right about the fancifulness. It had leaded glass windows of diamond panes. A corner turret climbed upward, too small for a stairway, perhaps even too small for a single chair, but it would flood the interior with light throughout the day. The door was darkly stout with swirling ironwork; if it was circular, it would have belonged in Hobbiton. The entry was framed by two ancient yew trees and looked like the entry to Tolkien's Mines of Moria but back in happier times. She inspected the door lintel but could see no elvish runes that might say, "Speak, friend, and enter." Still, it *felt* as if the words were there.

The roof was thickly thatched, creating deep curves and welcoming hollows. Atop the main thatch was more fanciful work making an ornate design. A pair of thatch ducks stood atop the peak and a line of thatch ducklings waddled across the ridge to join them. More birds.

A pheasant was perched at the other end, silhouetted against the achingly blue sky. She watched it for a long moment before she decided that it too was made of thatch. Just as she turned away, the pheasant burst to life and flew away.

It was as if her world, as if *she* was somehow…broken. Charleston, South Carolina, had always made sense. Sometimes an awful, painful sense, but she'd known how it worked. Now she had improbable, spirit guides offering her confusing signals that felt like messages if only she could interpret them. Pheasants and dusty White Knights. One who kept spooking her and the other who didn't.

"Go away, Aaron," she tried once more to banish his near-black eyes and slow smile from her thoughts.

Focus on the cottage. The garden was carpeted with yellow daffodils, white snowdrops, and purple aubrieta. Heavy coils of ancient rose vine climbed across the front facade. The lightest hint of green made it easy to imagine how spectacularly it would bloom in just a few months.

Jane looked up and down the lane. Cherry trees shone in brilliant displays of sun-catching pink, a beech and some maples just leafing out in bright green. A large stone trough stood on the other side of the road; a pipe jutted out of the low rise behind it and splashed water into a tub of stonework that probably predated the Norman Conquest of 1066. The water looked clear and cool, a natural spring.

Someone had placed a bench near the spring.

Unable to run any farther, she staggered over and sat down. The bench afforded a view past the cottage and out over the rolling grass-green hills. Fosse-on-the-Wold crested along the next rise. She sat for a long time gazing at the view and the cottage before she noticed the sign.

"For sale."

She couldn't understand the words, as if they were in a foreign language. Every time she'd seen those words in the last year, she'd lost something: her business, her townhouse, her parents' home and all of the memories from growing up there. In some strange fit of madness, she'd even sold her ten-year-old VW diesel and bought a one-way ticket to the Cotswolds. Not because she was planning to stay in England, but rather because she couldn't think of any reason to go back.

Yet this pretty little cottage had these same words on it.

"For sale."

She pulled out her phone, cleared her running app, and dialed the phone number.

~

"Now you're acting like an American."

"Maybe because I am one." Besides, wall building was hot work and Aaron didn't give a damn. He mopped his face with his wadded-up t-shirt, then tossed it aside. Trent was right, Aaron had never seen a shirtless Brit; but he was too hot to care. He dumped half his water bottle over his head and went back to work. He fetched a couple more rocks, barely resisting the urge to topple Trent from his perch.

The old man stood barely five-foot-six and looked like he was the direct descendant of a gnarled oak branch. Yet he rarely removed his jacket even when he was building wall at a rate that Aaron couldn't begin to match. The rock for a finished wall—at the standard one-and-a-half-meter height—weighed one ton per running meter. He'd seen Trent lay an unbelievable four meters in a day despite being a wizened little pain in the ass who was seventy if he was a day. Not only was he wiry with strength, but he also barely looked at the rocks he was placing. He'd done it for so many years, his hands simply knew what to do with every piece they picked up.

Aaron finished the base run for the next two meters and glanced at Trent for his approval. The old man nodded that, for once, he was good to continue.

Moving to the medium-sized stone pile, Aaron began working

on the outer walls. Every other row, he gathered handfuls of rubble and break-off to place between them. Trent insisted that these were as essential to the structural integrity as the two sides, every piece bigger than his thumb had to be consciously placed.

Aaron liked the rhythm of it. A special operations soldier lost himself in drilling the minutia until they became body memory. There was a certain peace in firing the same shot a hundred times, then turning his body fifteen degrees and firing another hundred rounds at the same point. Then another.

Aaron was able to step back mentally and let his hands do the work of sorting the scrap pieces from thumb- to palm-sized without really paying them any attention.

Usually when he was working a repetitive task, his mind went quiet. He could converse, but he enjoyed the silence of the morning. The only sounds were the slight shifting of the rock under Trent's ass as he raised and lowered his cigarette. A mourning dove calling with an unending *whoo-who-hoo-hoo,* always in the same notes. Silent blackbirds with sharp yellow beaks landed in a snappy flutter of wings to inspect his trench for worms.

But today they weren't comfortably distracting as they usually were. Instead he was—

"Still dreaming, lad."

"Go to hell, Trent."

"Probably," the old man chuckled. "If only for thinking I could teach an American to properly lay English stone."

Trent let him be as Aaron returned to raising the outer sides of the wall another few rows. It was rare for him not to have some correction to Aaron's handiwork. Even after three months, the man was still finding ways to improve Aaron's craft. There was a drive for perfection in the old man that he appreciated himself. Just like—

"Heard she's a fine looker."

Aaron bobbled the next stone.

Speaking of perfect.

He checked the slant of the stones, ever so slightly tipped to the outside. Slope of one in fifteen to shed water rather than gathering it into the center. Most stone walls used pinning stones, narrow wedges inside the wall to tip the stones outward. He and Trent both preferred the slower method of finding the right stone to maintain the slant.

"Though what such a girl would see in an American, one with a permanent grouch on, passes me by."

Aaron slammed the next half dozen stones into place.

By the depth of Trent's silence, he knew he was screwing up.

He flipped the stones back to the ground and began resetting them properly.

"There's some hope for you yet, lad," Trent proclaimed in one of his smoker's hoarse laughs.

Actually there wasn't. But as long as Aaron was the only one who knew that, it was okay.

JANE LIFTED the key from beneath the potted red geranium. The estate agent was off in some place called Lesser Tew and had told her she was free to poke around. Jane wasn't sure exactly where she was, but "The Springs Cottage" (the name on a small circular plaque beside the door) had meant something to the agent.

"Oh, you're just a couple hundred meters down Springs Lane from Fosse."

That was news to her. With the circles she'd run in, she could have been halfway to Oxford for all she knew.

Crossing under the two yew trees (still no sign saying, "Speak, friend, and enter"), she fit the key into the curiously modern lock. A skeleton key on a leather thong would be more appropriate. But the lock clicked easily and she was in.

The cottage was unfurnished. The floor was dark hardwood and softly uneven with centuries of wear. She'd been right, the corner turret was barely big enough for a small table to hold a bouquet of flowers, but it flooded the room with light. The main room had a massive stone fireplace. The lighting fixtures were tastelessly too modern and the kitchen and other amenities too ancient, but the cottage itself was incredible.

Up the small spiral stair hid two bedrooms to either side of a joined bath that could be made very cozy with a little effort.

The stairs continued upward in a narrow flight that led to a single space close under the roof that was all slants and angles. Some overlap of images had her checking the floor to make sure no handsome White Knight was sleeping there. He wasn't.

This would make a perfect office, just room for a desk and a few chairs. It had a large window that looked out over a lovely garden and a spectacular view of Fosse and the Cotswold hills. Two men were out front at the far end of the long front yard, one rebuilding the curving stone wall while another watched him. The watcher was a small man in a faded brown cap and jacket. She could only see the worker's back as he limped over to one of the piles, selected a stone, and carried it back to the wall. The finished curve would offer the perfect balance of enclosure yet openness to passersby on the footpath below.

She was barely aware of lifting the phone and pressing redial.

"Did you get in?" The real estate agent was cheerful on the line.

"Yes."

"Isn't it sweet?"

"Yes."

"I'm meeting someone there in a few hours to show it. We can talk more then if you'd like."

Jane imagined sitting in a floral armchair close by the window and watching the man building the wall, his bare back muscles flexing, arms lifting, hands grasping. His leg might have a limp but, as if he was made of contrasts, the rest of him that she could see was powerfully built. He looked so natural. He'd probably been doing it all his life.

"Hello?"

Natural. She'd never done anything naturally. Or even spontaneously. Every step of her career had been carefully mapped out, from the computer skills in high school and the business degree in college, to the masters in process engineering. Every job had been analyzed, weighed, measured.

"Are you still there?"

All she knew was that she never wanted to leave her imaginary chair. This room. This window.

A phone in her hand. A voice asking questions.

"You can cancel the appointment," she told the voice. "The Springs Cottage is already sold. I'm buying it."

After a quickly covered squawk of surprise, the man started saying something about time, place, and—

"I'll be here," Jane hung up and pocketed the phone.

She watched the man building the wall. Watched the way he selected, placed, adjusted, and moved on.

Moved on.

Is that what she was doing?

Moving on?

Or was she having a nervous breakdown?

For the life of her she couldn't tell.

"NOW THERE'S A LIKELY ONE," Trent said from his perch atop the rock pile.

"What are you talking about, old man?" Aaron didn't bother looking up from the wall. If he focused on that, he didn't have to focus on how Jane Tully refused to walk out of his thoughts as she had out of his room.

"Old, but not blind," Trent poked his cigarette toward the house.

Aaron turned to see Jane herself walking down the garden

path from the cottage. She stumbled to a halt as she recognized him.

"Birds," her voice little more than a whisper of shock. Whether it was a shock or a curse, he couldn't quite tell, but he understood the feeling.

"No, actually, Aaron."

"Aaron," Jane repeated it as if she'd never heard the name before. She raised her hands and pressed them to her red cheeks.

"Told you. I can spot 'em still, just fine," Trent was practically crowing with delight. "She's the lark from the wedding, isn't she?"

"I hear you talking, Trent, but no one's listening."

He certainly wasn't.

Aaron couldn't look away from the shining apparition before him. He'd thought that Jane wearing only her underwear in the moonlight of his room had been a revelation. That was nothing compared to this.

He'd assumed that she attained her fine form from careful dieting and a personal trainer named Sven. But in Lycra leggings and some clinging, high-tech tank top, her body was a masterful statement. That stunning flow of blonde hair that had graced her shoulders last night was back in a cheery ponytail. Her green eyes hidden by dark sunglasses wrapped so tightly to her temples that they almost looked implanted. They emphasized her high cheekbones and fine features. Her face was flushed with running.

She was wired up with music player, headphones, exercise tracker on one wrist and an oversized runner's watch on the other that probably did lap, split, and who knew what all. Even her shoes looked top of the line. Jane Tully looked like a living, breathing ad for a sports magazine—an impossible distance from the exquisite blonde at last night's society wedding.

There was a time he'd have welcomed the sight. A special operations soldier did a lot of running—with gear that was built for rougher use, but the joy of the pounding miles was the same. Not anymore. Now she was a shining example of everything he no longer was. Before, he could run anyone into the ground. Now, he couldn't even jog.

"You're staring again, Aaron," Jane's voice was as steady as the stone still clenched in his hands.

"I am?" Didn't mean he could stop.

"You are," Trent offered on a short laugh.

"You are," Jane agreed.

"Well, if the dress was good, this is spectacular."

She kicked at the dirt a few times, getting dust on her immaculate sneakers.

Aaron couldn't think of what to say next.

"Youth is wasted on the wrong people," Trent growled.

"*It's a Wonderful Life,*" he and Jane named the movie together.

"What are you talking about?"

Aaron looked at Trent and saw his confusion. "Never mind." He turned back to Jane, hoping that she hadn't disappeared in his momentary lapse of judgment in looking away.

She hadn't.

"You're a stonemason."

Aaron nodded, ignoring Trent's snort of derision.

"Did you build walls in Vermont as well?"

"Yes." Could he make less use of an opening?

"You're a stonemason named Aaron Mason. Don't you think that was being a little too obvious?"

He shrugged. Yes, when pushed, he apparently could do even less.

"Why are you limping? Did you hurt yourself?"

He barely managed even a nod this time. Nine 7.62 mm rounds in the leg from an AK-47. Three broken bones, a shattered knee, a couple of through-and-through meat shots, and a severed artery that almost killed him right there in goddamn Yemen. The docs had bolted his knee back together as well as they could. They said it would be fine, it would just take time to get strong—like a year. Meanwhile he could get around well enough, but had to do his rehab exercises half an hour twice a day. Or he was supposed to.

"He doesn't pay more mind, he'll be dropping that ruddy stone, pardon my language ma'am, on his foot. Then he'll be having something else to hop about by my reckoning."

"You didn't limp last night."

And here it came. Aaron turned and carried his rock to the wall, snugging it down into the dirt, tight against the other two.

"Mind your line," Trent snapped out.

Aaron had heard it a thousand times over the last three months. To build a wall, you ripped down the old one, cut a trench as deep as your fingertips to your wrist, then built up the quoin, the cheek or finished end of the wall. Normally a set of strings were stretched from there to a batter frame, a wooden form at the finish point that matched the exact profile of the wall, and every stone must almost brush one or the other of those outside strings.

But this was his first curving wall, making a great arc between the footpath and the garden. No stretched strings here. He knelt, keeping his curses about the pain to himself, and sighted down the curve of the trench that Trent had made him fuss over for days until he was satisfied with its shape. The last rocks fit perfectly in the final shape.

"My line is fine."

Trent just shook his head in disgust. The old man creaked to his feet, muttering imprecations to Saint Stephen, the patron saint of stonemasons, then, stepping over the wall, headed up the footpath and into town.

"You seem to have upset him." Jane still stood in the yard.

"Nothing new," Aaron shrugged.

"How did you hurt yourself?"

"I upset an al-Shabaab militiaman in the Tihamah in Yemen. Worst place in the world you can imagine. Have you ever been to Miami in the summer?"

She nodded cautiously, her eyes shot wide.

"The Tihamah region is worse than that."

Jane didn't even manage a nod this time.

Shit! He'd done it. Exactly what he'd been so careful not to mention to anyone all these months. Fosse-on-the-Wold had been his fresh start, his clean slate. And he'd blown it in an instant for a woman he barely knew. Couldn't he have just lied and said he'd dropped a rock on himself? A wall had collapsed and shattered his knee? Lied and said that he'd be fine…as soon as she was gone.

In disgust, he turned away, knelt, and gathered another stone. He gave her time to escape, checking the lay of the stone carefully, nudging it until he was happy with the line of the curve he was creating. Unable to sustain the kneeling, he finally rolled down to a sitting position and dug a thumb into his damn spasming muscle.

"You're still here."

Jane nodded.

How did such a simple name describe such a woman?

"Why did you hide it? Last night?"

"I'm sorry. That wasn't honest of me." He was sorry for so much.

"That's an evasion," that odd flat tone of the pub was back.

Now it was his turn to nod. It *was* an evasion. Not a chance of him explaining that he'd been some awestruck boy trying to impress a beautiful woman when there was never really a chance of it working.

Aaron managed to climb back to his feet and moved to select the next rock. He made a show of digging through the pile before selecting the next one for the base layer. He placed it and went for another. He'd laid four feet of base layer before he finally saw her move off, a shadow no longer cast upon the grass, back up the yard and around to the lane side of the cottage.

He watched her go, the light step of an experienced runner. Her ponytail swinging back and forth as if brushing the dust of

Aaron Mason off her shoulders. Good for her. She'd be better off without the likes of him vainly hoping for more than she'd ever be willing to give.

Aaron turned back to the wall to check his line, but the wall didn't seem to matter anymore. Who gave a bloody goddamn if the curve went a few degrees one way or the other? Why did the wall get to have a proper permanent place? How had it earned the right? Had it trained, fought, killed? Had it—

He recognized the darkness of the incoming spiral but couldn't do a thing to divert it. He stepped over the wall and out into the field. Out of sight. Away from wall, woman, and himself. He collapsed behind an oak tree, out of sight of anyone except a flock of goddamn sheep.

The darkness came and wrapped about him. An old, familiar friend that sank its claws into his soul.

But something was different this time. There was a glimmer of light in the gloom, a voice softer than the malevolent shades and demons that sought to consume him.

A voice wrapped in golden hair and sunlight. Even walking away from him, the Faerie Queen Jane Tully shone like a candle in his personal darkness.

CHAPTER 4

Jane knew it was a mistake, but Fosse-on-the-Wold was a one-pub town and she had nowhere else to go. She'd avoided the town all day until even the tea rooms were closed, leaving only the one place for food.

Staying at the manor wasn't an option. Even with her sister and the Third Worm of Evenston gone, Worms One and Two were still in residence. Worm One was between wives and Worm Two didn't care that he wasn't. The earl had absented himself somewhere deep within the manor but there were still plenty of guests in residence for the drunken celebrations to continue even without the bride and groom.

After meeting the estate agent and making an offer, she had nowhere else to go. The agent had suggested that Jane should also offer to rent it immediately on a month-to-month basis so that the owner would have immediate income while the sale was negotiated, but even that would take a few days to go through.

She'd looked for B&Bs around town, but they were all full due to the pretty spring weather. A few suggested she ask at The Queen's Guard—her least preferred choice.

Finally, parched, hungry, and needing to escape Fosse Manor

while she still could, she retreated to The Queen's Guard. There was no sign of Aaron and, with careful timing, she managed to acquire an emptying table out of the sightline from the fireside table where she'd met him the first time.

Bridget delivered a menu. She wasn't hungry, but pointed to the first item and asked for tea as well. Definitely no beer tonight.

The tea arrived quickly, a pot massive enough to fill multiple mugs. There was no way to estimate how many times it would fill the porcelain teacup. There was also a small chilled pitcher of milk and a glass jar filled with lumpy white and brown sugar cubes with a set of dainty sugar tweezers. She kept forgetting that tea was something that the English did not take casually. She could learn to enjoy that.

When the meal came, she could only stare at it suspiciously. "What's that?"

"It's what you ordered, love." Bridget's smile said that she was enjoying the moment. Aaron would be pleased to know that there was no uniquely wonderful bond between women working in Jane's favor here.

"Help me out?"

"It's whitebait and chips. Small whole fish, battered and deep fried. And chips, what you'd be calling French fries. I gave you tartar but there are them as like brown sauce—though I can't see them as being in their right minds as this is fish, not meat." Bridget's amusement continued to grow. "Go on now. Try one. They're long past biting back."

Jane took a fish no bigger than her pinkie by the tail. She ignored the fact that it seemed to be watching her through the breading, dunked it in the tartar, and bit it off. It was tender and gently fish-flavored, with a satisfying crunch about it. It was good. She swallowed carefully. Her stomach didn't seem to mind her first solid food of the day either.

"Hard night last night?" The waitress didn't seem to be in a hurry to run off despite the thickness of the evening crowd.

"Today wasn't exactly a winner either," Jane agreed. There was the cottage, but there was also the hard rebuff from Aaron. What had she done to offend him? Actually, she could think of several things. Drunken slob who'd dragged him into the lion's den. Then she'd toyed with him (it wasn't like her but it was the only thing that explained the drunken partial memory of his kiss). And how had she thanked him this morning? By running away at her first chance. "Actually, mostly an awful day."

"Whoof!," Bridget agreed with some sympathy. "Don't you know it. The morning after is never a good one, is it? Always seems worth it at the time though. A good night's rest on your ear will set you to rights."

Jane decided it was the best opening she was going to get, "You don't have a room available by any chance?"

"On the weekend? What with the big fancy do of a wedding in town? Not ruddy likely. But I'll check with Hal."

Jane also wanted to ask about Aaron, but couldn't figure out how to do so before Bridget moved off. Maybe she could find a sleeping bag and stay in that fairy-tale cottage.

Away from Aaron. Except he was there at the cottage as well. Or had been.

By the time she'd dared look out the windows again, Aaron was gone. The unfinished wall mocked her.

Normally when a man rejected her so thoroughly, she turned tail and ran. It was so much easier that way. Don't fight the traces, just let them go entirely. But even as she'd walked away from him this morning, she'd known it was wrong.

Any normal man, she would have dismissed as yet another abysmal Jane Tully failure. Aaron, however, had already proved himself to her last night. He'd taken no advantage of her state. He'd taken care of her. Aaron had protected her from the Worm Sons (his very apropos name for them still made her smile), her sister (a feat of unimaginable magnitude), and herself (despite her attempt to dive headlong into total drunken destruction).

He—

"What the hell are you doing here?" Aaron, of course. And angry enough that he'd lost any hint of English. He was pure, Vermont, pissed male. For some reason she found that comforting.

"Eating something called whitebait."

"It's a fish."

"Noticed that all on my own."

He grunted. He didn't look any happier, but at least she'd stymied him back to alpha-male grunts. That she knew how to handle.

She topped up her tea, added a splash of milk, and selected her next bit of fish as if nothing was amiss.

Without asking, he plummeted into the seat across the table and thumped his beer on the table. That's when she spotted her planning error—she was out of sight from the fireplace and the door, but not the bar. She'd remember that in the future.

She saw the wince as he shifted in his seat.

"Does it hurt a lot?"

He shrugged.

"Because of your work today?" She certainly wasn't going to sit here in stone silence at her own table simply because Mr. Unsmooth had turned into Mr. Grumpy.

"Some. Last night mostly."

"Because you were hiding it from me. Because you didn't want me to see you as less of a man." It hadn't taken long to figure that out. She didn't make it a question.

He didn't argue.

"Are you always such a straight shooter?"

"Used to be," that wince looked far deeper than anything merely physical.

She couldn't stop the smile at the next image, even though she could see the pain on his face. In his eyes.

He inspected her cautiously, then sipped his beer. "Okay, hit me with it. But that smile better not end up with me going to another wedding."

"Promise," she raised her right hand as solemnly as any Girl Scout.

He tipped his glass as if to signal he was as ready as he'd ever be.

"Your past sucked," Jane felt like an idiot the moment she said it. How had she assumed she knew anything about him?

"No," he casually sipped his beer as if this was somehow a normal conversation. "My past was awesome. My present sucks. Future doesn't look exactly awe inspiring."

"Well, I'll up you a past, a present, and no obvious future." It still took her breath away just how much she'd lost how fast. Parents, almost-fiancé, and now...everything else. Job, career, home, confidence—all down the toilet in one neat, agonizing, year-long flush. Maybe that's what the cottage was about, an attempt to plug the drain before anything else slid down it. There wasn't much left to slide.

That earned one of his more sympathetic grunts, "Sorry to hear that."

And there were those eyes she remembered from last night. The ones that had watched her so carefully through the whole wedding. Every time she'd turned around she'd caught him watching her. Dark eyes, observant, thoughtful. She wondered if caring lurked there as well or was that simply her inane, misguided, ever-hopeful inner self being ridiculously naive?

"I'm still waiting on the joke."

She raised her teacup and tapped it against his beer, "We make a hell of a pair, don't we?"

No laugh of acknowledgement on that one. But the tip of his beer and wry grimace said plenty.

~

AARON DIDN'T KNOW what to do with the anger that was building inside him.

Tamp it down, soldier! Except he was no longer a soldier.

What the hell had he been fighting for if the world gave women like Jane an unhappy life and sisters like Debbie?

God damn it! It just wasn't right!

Not that he could do shit about it anymore.

Yeah, let me toast to two lives sucking, because that's so much better than only one.

He could feel the Black Demon. The one born in the heat of the Yemeni desert, that had flown with him on the combat-search-and-rescue bird, and hovered so near while the pretty black paramedic had fought to save his life. It had been such a strangely intimate thing—his life-or-death moment that they'd shared so closely—yet he'd never even found out her name. Never saw her again to thank her. He'd gone to sleep in transit to some carrier, listening to the heavy beat of the helo's rotors and watching her up to her elbows in his blood. And woken up as they shipped him out of Landstuhl, Germany, headed stateside for Walter Reed.

But the demon didn't come. Maybe it couldn't touch him here. He'd mentally built up The Queen's Guard pub as a bastion of safety—which even worked...occasionally.

No, the real reason was obvious. The Black Demon was repulsed by the light of the Faerie Queen. It was ridiculous to make Jane Tully his talisman, but it was hard to resist because it was true.

Bridget came over and the two women chatted about something that seemed to cheer Jane until she shone even brighter.

"Is that okay with you?" Jane asked him a question directly.

"Is what okay with me?"

Bridget and Jane gave him the same look. Not quite the same, Jane had the decency to not roll her eyes at him.

"I can't stay at the manor house—the Worm brothers are still in residence."

Bridget laughed aloud at that.

"Damn straight," he agreed. If one of those slimeballs tried to touch her, he'd cut their damn dicks off and that was *before* he ripped their guts out.

"But someone just had their holiday cut short and is headed back to London now. So Hal has a spare room here, if that's okay with you?"

Aaron decided that his knee would not appreciate him dancing a jig. The Faerie Queen resident in The Queen's Guard? Even for a few nights? Too perfect to be dreamed of. The Black Demon didn't stand a chance. He'd given her the cold shoulder at the cottage wall for her own sake, yet still she was here. That must mean something.

He knew he was setting himself up for the long fall, but one glance at Jane's happy green eyes, sparkling in the pub's soft light, was too powerful to deny.

"Sure. Sounds fine," he managed past the dry throat that even the Donnington SBA couldn't slake.

"I have to go get my things. There isn't much, but it would be easier if you..." Jane trailed off and glanced uncertainly down toward his lower extremities though the table was between them.

"I can walk and carry just fine."

She winced and Bridget looked ready to kick his ass. He hadn't mean it to come out as a growl but it did anyway.

"I'm glad to help," he sounded better on the second attempt. "If you don't mind me letting my knee do what it wants to."

"You hereby have my permission to limp in my presence at any time," Jane delivered her benediction regally. She was so perfect that he couldn't help smiling.

Despite a pleasant enough dinner together, the walk had started awkwardly. Jane could feel herself trying to not watch Aaron's limp and she could feel Aaron feeling her not watching, which made her feel…like a bewildered fool.

But by the time they reached the shadowed footpath to the manor, she'd grown used to it. It wasn't like he was horribly deformed (which was how he made it sound). Aaron simply limped.

"How did it happen?" Only too late did she realize what an intrusive question that was. "I'm sorry. You don't have to—"

"Have you ever read a Houthi flag?"

"Houthi?" Then she recalled a news item before she could sound too naive. "Yemen. Rebels. Their flag has words?"

"*God Is Great, Death to America, Death to Israel, Curse on the Jews, Victory to Islam.*"

"Not very friendly."

"We were in-country to clean out the head man of a terrorist camp that they were cosponsoring with al-Qaeda. The simple raid became a fifty-minute firefight. I was second to last man out."

"Who was last?"

"The female medic who saved my life. I got shot up at the last moment by a twelve-year-old kid who picked up his dead father's AK-47 when no one had eyes on him. One of the helicopter crew chiefs killed the kid. At least I was spared that."

Jane didn't know what to say. Her dusty stonemason was so much more than she'd ever imagined.

"Were you a SEAL or one of those other things?"

That earned her a brief smile despite the grim topic. "One of those 'other things.' Sergeant in Delta Force on loan to the SAS for a year. I spent an amazing year fighting beside the best soldiers the Brits ever produced. Delta was originally based on the SAS and the two worked together pretty closely. Still do." His last words were filled with that pain again.

Straight shooter?

Used to be.

The pain of being an outsider.

"You miss it."

"Like breathing."

Jane thought about that. "I've never had anything good enough to miss that much."

"What do you do?"

She wasn't ready to answer that, but neither could she deny his honesty. The shadowed oak-and-beech tunnel of the footpath was ending. Unable to face her own past in the bright evening sunlight, she stumbled to a halt only a few steps from the end of the shadows. The bird song, which she hadn't been noticing, roared to life around her. She startled as a pigeon bolted out of the hedgerow and noisily flew off from no more than an arm's length away.

Aaron didn't flinch in the slightest though the bird launched from close by his shoulder. Nerves of steel. He stopped and waited, listening. Since when did men listen?

"I was a project manager."

She saw his look of uncertainty.

"I know. The most non-specific job title ever created. I specialize, *specialized,*" and she could feel her own version of Aaron's pain at the past tense, "in fixing complex office systems. Sometimes computers, often workflow, always personnel."

"What little I know of you, I'm guessing you were good at it. What happened?"

"I co-owned a very small, very lean company with a woman I'd always thought of as a mentor. It turned out that we had very different definitions of the word integrity. Suddenly I was alone at the center of breached contracts, massive debts, and a never-ending stream of undeliverable promises that I hadn't even known about."

And still she could see Kathie's face exactly one week before it all broke apart. *I just got an offer from Nintendo for a full-time job that I couldn't resist, but you're doing great. I know you'll knock 'em dead, darling.* And Kathie had been gone. She'd thought seriously about calling Nintendo to warn them of the snake in their midst, but had finally taken the high road out of town.

"I lost the business, the career, and any interest in ever doing that job again," Jane could feel her voice go flat but couldn't stop herself.

"When was this?" Aaron's soft question drew her back. He had listened. He had heard.

He might be the first person who ever had, at least since Mama died.

Kathie had betrayed her and left. Her parents lost to a car crash six months before—Mama surviving only long enough to make her promise to look after her sister. Larry the almost-fiancé professor had never been much for listening to anyone talk except himself. She'd been too much of a workaholic to have any real friends. Her sister Debbie was…Debbie.

"I closed the final bank account last Wednesday, reported the business closed to the state and IRS tax bureaus Thursday, and caught the redeye from Charleston, South Carolina, to Heathrow for the Friday wedding." And it was too much, too raw. She tried to hold it in, but couldn't. Not from the man watching her so intently—anchored in some impossibly deep core of inner stillness. Definitely not from herself.

AARON DIDN'T KNOW much about women who cried, but back in high school, Mary—the bridesmaid he'd met at the wedding he'd crashed—had taught him one thing to do. She'd had a hard family: alcoholic and seriously dysfunctional (she'd had to explain that). His own dad was a dairy farmer and his mom a nurse—both steady and practical. Not the warmest people, but not cold either.

When Jane began crying, he didn't judge her for it—the pain

was too obvious, too raw. Instead, he took a step in and pulled her into his arms.

Mary had been right, a crying woman wanted to be held.

Jane kept her arms crossed over her chest as if her heart hurt, but she wasn't pushing him away. Instead, she lay her face on his shoulder and wept. He was glad for the distance her crossed arms enforced between their bodies, but she still felt incredible as she sagged against him. He rubbed his hands up and down her back, appreciating its fine lines and the fitness of the musculature currently shuddering with the sobs. She wasn't making a big deal of it, no weeping and wailing for Jane Tully, just crying quietly.

He'd never understood why it made him feel so strong to hold a crying woman. Strong was sliding into a denied zone with nothing but your wits, night-vision goggles, and an HK416 combat rifle. But holding a woman while she cried made him feel very—as she'd called it—male. He never felt so *male* as when holding a woman in pain. And holding Jane Tully was a whole new dimension on that one.

Slowly she ran dry, managed a shuddering breath, then another.

"Thank you," she whispered against his neck.

"No worries."

"That's Australian, not British," Jane's whisper tickled against his skin.

He shrugged. It was, but he'd adopted it years before because he liked the feel of it.

"You're going to have to decide who you are someday."

Aaron knew exactly who he was—who he had been. But she was right as usual. Who he was *now*? Present tense? He'd be damned if he knew.

"You can let go now."

"Do I have to?" No longer crying, Jane was no less pleasant to hold close. Her long fall of hair ran slick over the backs of his hands as they traveled up and down her back. The feel of—

"No, you don't have to. But you should."

So he did. And felt the emptiness in his arms immediately.

Jane was red-eyed as he wiped away the last of her tears for her.

The intimacy of the moment was too reminiscent of when she'd wiped the cake icing off his nose and chin last night beneath the moonlight. He stepped back, running into the hedgerow and once more upsetting the nesting pigeon who had returned to its depths while Jane cried.

"I got your shirt all wet," she dabbed at his shoulder with her bare fingers.

Aaron glanced down at the small damp patch. "I've had worse." For one thing, it wasn't the dark red of fresh blood. "I think I'll survive this wound."

Before she could ask what he meant by that and he was forced to tell her something she wouldn't want to hear, he offered her his elbow. She slipped her hand into place and a calm slid over him. Somehow everything was all right as long as she held onto him.

Arm in arm they proceeded along the footpath and out into the sunlit backyard of the grand manor. Sure, it was an architectural hodgepodge, but the place was growing on him.

JANE HAD HOPED to slip in, pack, and slip away again.

The first two stages happened easily. The party had migrated out onto the front lawn, leaving the manor itself quiet and peaceful. It had been odd packing her clothes with Aaron in the room but, she rationalized, he'd already seen her bra and panties in far more compromising circumstances than being moved from drawer to suitcase. Still, he tactfully moved to a window and stared out at the grounds.

She would miss the view. There probably weren't any rooms in the manor with a bad view, but this room looked down over the flower garden. Beyond a boundary stone wall, that she now had a little more appreciation for, sheep pastures rolled down the hill to where a lazy river meandered along the valley. On the opposite side, more of the same. Farm buildings, limestone houses, and the bigger town of Stow-on-the-Wold perched atop the next hill just a mile away. It was a grand view; her cottage's (she couldn't help thinking of it that way already) view was smaller, less formal, yet more welcoming.

She packed fast. Her job, her *former* job, had included at least twice-monthly travel so she had it down. And her belongings were now few enough that they fit in two small suitcases and a not much larger storage unit in South Carolina. Without the job, or even the prospect of one, she'd sold her townhouse and her parents' house. The housing market had turned and she was now very well situated, other than not having anywhere to live except an English pub and no idea of what came next.

Running shoes, wedding shoes, and hiking shoes—not even sandals. She would have left the wedding attire behind (she certainly wouldn't need that again), but she didn't want to perpetrate it on the earl. Maybe she'd have a ritual burning of it later. It was too bad, she'd liked it on first sight and bought it on impulse a year ago, then never had an occasion to wear it. Now it had been on twice: once for Debbie's wedding and once for her shameful morning-after scurry through town. Unable to relocate Aaron's footpath back to the manor, she'd had to wear it among the dog walkers and early joggers as she'd followed the main road to reach the manor's long driveway.

Then as she folded it away, she remembered the way Aaron had looked at her wearing the dress. Maybe she would keep it, for a while anyway.

Once she was packed and they'd both double-checked the room and bath, she was all for bolting. But, at the front door she'd spotted a maid and inquired about leaving a note of thanks for the earl.

~

AARON KNEW they were in trouble just by the sound.

The maid had gone off quietly on soft shoes, leaving them while she went to fetch something they could use to leave a note.

The front hall was a three-story gothic-arched monster. Had the wedding been rained out, it could have been held here at the foot of the two staircases of dark stone that swept down either side of the hall from the upper story. There would have been plenty of room to spare with only a hundred guests. Massive paintings, dark with age, adorned towering walls of stone. High windows, faced to capture the midday light, were turning subtly orange as the sun ducked away to the west.

He offered Jane his arm for a quick turn about the room and couldn't believe when she took it. It was as if today had never happened. As if he hadn't been such an asshole when she'd just been trying to be nice. They were just up the grand central passage far enough that he couldn't see who was coming down the stairs when the sound started.

But the sharp staccato punch of high heels on stone was a sound like no other. Last night he'd cataloged the rhythm as well.

"Incoming! Brace yourself," was all he had time to whisper to Jane before Debbie, now Debbie Evenston, came off the bottom step and spotted them. She sauntered across the hall toward them like she owned the place.

"What do you see in *her?*" Debbie's voice was smooth and oily and tried to wrap around him like a snake.

"Good evening, Ms. Evenston," Aaron made a slight bow but knew better than to offer his hand this time. He could see the choice register and the fury rise.

She turned to fire a barb at Jane, but that wasn't going to happen.

"I'd have thought you'd be off on your honeymoon by now," he sidetracked her before she could launch.

"Geoffie's plane had a breakdown. We could have flown first class this morning, but who wants to do that, and all those flight changes. It's fixed and we're just going now. He keeps it just up the road, you know."

Just keep talking, Debbie. That's what you're good at.

"They *are* holding the yacht for us. We'll catch up with it at Portofino. It's the *Immaculate*. Two-hundred-and-sixty-feet long. Though I assume you don't know her."

"I rarely travel on something so small." He typically deployed off littoral combat ships in the four-hundred-foot range, destroyers over five hundred, or carriers up in the thousand-foot-plus category. Aaron managed to keep his face straight.

Jane didn't. Her snort of laughter at her sister's expense probably didn't earn her many points. Jane knew his was ex-military, but Debbie didn't.

Unable to leave it alone, he continued. "Of course the *Immaculate* was formerly the *Elite Voyager III*. After she was pirated, they changed the name and shifted her up from the Caribbean for resale." He hadn't been part of that takedown, but Delta had studied the bloody results of sending in a standard boarding team against armed Colombian drug pirates.

Debbie's face blanched white though she covered quickly. He watched her gear up to take one more slice at Jane, glance over at him, then think better of it. She turned on her heel and stalked away without another word.

"I don't think she likes me very much," he whispered to Jane. "She isn't even offering me a departing ass wiggle like last night."

Jane laughed again, loudly enough that Debbie slammed the front door only moments later. "Perhaps not. But I'm finding that I like you more and more, Mr. Mason."

Jane couldn't believe her reprieve or the unexpected source of it. Aaron had handled Debbie with all the aplomb of a corporate CEO. Yes, she could get to like him *very* much. There'd be hell to pay later but, whatever the price, it would be completely worth it.

Moments later the maid reappeared and they were whisked into the Earl of Evenston's office.

"You're leaving us so soon?" He was on his feet in a moment and coming around the desk.

"I thought it best," Jane couldn't remember if she'd been in this room on last night's mid-wedding tour.

It was a fine space without being a grand one. No extra walls had been knocked out to make the room more expansive. It held a large oaken desk, a small circle of red leather chairs around the inevitable large fireplace, and a large window offering an intimate view of the flower garden that she had overlooked from her room above. Dark wood floors and stone predominated, though large bookcases invited her to select a volume and curl up in one of the chairs by the fireplace.

"Your office is very cozy."

"Thank you. That was my intent. It reminds me that what is important is being comfortable, not wrapped up in excess."

Jane kept any thought about the excesses of a twenty-six-bedroom manor to herself.

His laugh boomed out easily, telling her that she wished her emotions were less obvious.

"Sit for a moment, please," he waved them into chairs.

Aaron offered a microscopic shrug to go with flow, so the three of them settled together about the unlit fireplace.

"I'm actually a simple man in many ways, though you may not believe it. Very successful, I grant, but I am not my youngest son."

"That's a blessing," then Jane slapped a hand over her mouth, but the earl's look of chagrin granted her the point. Then his easy smile broke out and his blue-gray eyes were filled with amusement.

Aaron's cross between a snort and a chuckle made her feel only a little better for her indiscretion.

"Were my eldest son not happily engaged to a doctor, I could recommend him to your acquaintance, but I see that I'm too late for that already. You have found your stonemason."

"*My* stonemason?" Jane was unsure of quite what that meant. "We only met last night…your lordship." What was the right thing to call an earl? "He was kind enough to help me through a…difficult evening. I apologize for the misdirection."

"Lord is correct. But please call me Conrad."

Earl Conrad? Not a chance. He was too imposing a figure for first names.

"So, young man," he turned his attention to Aaron. "What possible reason can you provide me that I should trust an American apprentice stonemason with the attentions of this fine woman?"

Jane tried not to blush at the compliment. As far as she could recall, she barely knew the earl and hadn't exactly been presenting her best side for most of that time.

"Because, sir, I will defend her against anyone wishing her harm. Anyone."

Jane's ears were ringing, as if she'd just been struck like some brass church bell. She couldn't have heard that right.

Everything shifted into slow motion as she turned to face him.

Aaron's dark gaze remained on the earl for a long moment, and then slowly turned to meet hers.

He had slouched in the chair, his right leg extended out as if to ease it.

His fingers were interlaced over his flat stomach.

Completely at ease. As if they were all just telling stories and he wasn't trained as one of the most lethal warriors in any military.

When he looked at her, he wasn't Aaron Mason the stonemason. He was Sergeant Aaron Mason of Delta Force and the SAS, and he had just promised that he would defend her no matter what. To the death? The way he'd said it, that was clearly what he'd meant. From any lesser man it would be a boast or a throw-away line. But from him it was one of the most dangerous threats a man could make.

How could he just say such a thing?

About *her?*

He nodded once, solidly, as if he could read her question. As if confirming that, for her, he was willing to—

She really wished she was the sort of woman who fainted. The moment would be so much easier if that were the case.

~

AARON HAD BEEN TRAINED to protect the innocent.

That both was and wasn't Jane Tully. She hadn't been trained for his world, though it was clear that she'd found ways to survive hard times of her own. Still, there were hard truths he would face again if necessary in order to protect her.

He supposed he should be shocked by what he'd just said.

Jane clearly was. If she didn't start breathing again in the next twenty seconds, he'd have to remind her so that she didn't pass out.

But Aaron wasn't shocked. He'd spoken simple truth. And on consideration, it wasn't just his training that had made him speak. He would defend Jane against all comers because she was that special and the world needed as many people like her as it could get.

The earl didn't look surprised either, instead he looked thoughtful.

"I'm inclined to believe you, young man."

"You should, sir."

He heard Jane take a shuddering breath, then another. In his peripheral vision he could see that her color was slowly returning.

"Is she in need of such protection?"

"In a proper world, we'll never need to answer that question, sir."

If the earl thought he could somehow see into Aaron's soul by staring, he was welcome to try. Aaron had faced down too many drill instructors, officers, and just plain rude buggers to be bothered by the earl's assessment.

"I think I could get to like you, Mr. Mason."

"He's—"

He glanced over at Jane just as she bit off her sentence. He'd rather leave his past behind and thankfully she appeared to understand that.

"I find he's very likeable," Jane covered.

When she didn't add anything, it was Aaron's turn to be surprised.

Not "Despite..." or "Except for..."

After how much of an asshole he'd been this morning, he didn't even know why she was speaking to him, much less calling him likeable.

Likeability had never really been high on his list of personal achievements. In Delta and the SAS, trustworthy was by far the key trait. You could be a goddamn son of a bitch but, if you always had someone's back covered, you were in good. Close buddies he hadn't fought battles with? He couldn't think of a one. Friends from high school, who he had a couple beers with when home on leave, were wrapped up in lives that he understood as little as they understood his. Now, a permanent civilian, he wished he'd listened harder to what they had to say.

In the last twenty-four hours he'd lied to Jane about being whole, twice kissed the crap out of her when she was blind drunk, given her a rude brush-off this morning, and was only waiting to see what he'd do to her next with his clumsiness.

A soldier can't afford mistakes.

Maybe he'd finally found a single good thing about no longer being a soldier. Mistakes were no longer likely to cost him his life, only his self-respect.

The earl looked away first but there was something in his smile that told Aaron that he'd somehow lost this round as well.

"Are you all packed?" The earl returned his attention to Jane.

"Two suitcases," she managed, still sounding breathless. "In the hall. Aaron offered to help me carry them to the inn. The pub. I've taken a room at The Queen's Guard."

"Carry them? Neither of you has a vehicle?"

Aaron had a key for Trent's work truck, but hadn't thought to fetch it.

The earl picked up the phone and dialed, "Bring around the bronze Cooper, would you?"

By the time they reached the front door, a bronze-colored MINI Cooper was waiting for them. It was a four-seat convertible with the top down. A quick glance at the odometer revealed it had been driven less than twenty miles—barely enough to unload it from a car carrier and test it.

"It's yours for as long as you're in the UK," the earl waved a hand at it so negligently that Aaron wondered if he kept a small fleet of brand-new vehicles on hand for just such moments.

"Oh, I couldn't," Jane was shaking her head.

"Nonsense," the earl lifted one of her suitcases into the back-seat with surprising ease for an elderly man, though it *was* the smaller of the two. "Unless of course you'd rather drive the pink Ferrari?"

Jane just shook her head. Her ponytail broke free. It looked as if she tried to shake it forward to hide behind, but it stubbornly insisted on remaining down her back, leaving her blush for all to see.

"You don't like pink Ferraris?" The earl's tone was teasing.

"It's my sister's."

"Do you think she'd miss it?"

"Probably not," Jane admitted. "I know she can't drive a manual. She can barely drive an automatic."

"Helpless women," the old man shook his head sadly. "Please tell me you aren't a helpless woman."

That was one of the *last* words Aaron would ever apply to Jane Tully.

In answer, Jane stalked up to the left-side door and yanked it open. After glaring at it for a moment, she slammed it shut and walked around to the right-hand-side driver's door.

It had taken Aaron weeks to get used to which side of the vehicle to use in England, something that had tickled his SAS buddies no end.

Aaron shared a smile with the earl.

"Stop smirking and get in. Unless you want to walk back," Jane didn't even look up at him as she belted in.

Aaron lifted the other suitcase into the back, then slid into the passenger seat.

"Taking your life into your hands, young man?" The earl asked him with a broad wink as he closed Aaron's door and waved them off.

It was only as they were underway down the gravel drive that he caught the earl's double meaning: getting in a car with a driver fresh out of America, and doing anything he could to be with Jane Tully—even for just a little while.

Maybe it finally *was* time he took his life into his own hands.

CHAPTER 5

Her first night in the pub was a revelation. Jane couldn't remember another evening like it when the world simply slowed down. Her life had never been that way that she could recall…ever.

She came downstairs after settling in. The evening had progressed enough that while parts of the pub were still active, others were dimly lit and full of comfortable shadows. She ended up joining Aaron, sitting by the fire, his bad leg propped up on a chair.

In another chair sat Hal the barman, with Snoop the aging spaniel sprawled in doggy dogg heaven across his lap. Hal wore a Winnie-the-Pooh tie with the explanation that he'd recently been through Paddington Station. When Aaron pointed out it should be a Paddington Bear tie then, Hal merely shook his head in dismay at Aaron's naivete. The two men spoke easily, with long silences while they just watched the flames.

Bridget and a few other helpers had managed the last of the on-going service.

A few locals sat by the fire with them, some nursing a beer. None of them were in a rush. How different from the life she'd left behind barely forty-eight hours ago, a life where there were never enough minutes in the day so she worked half the night as well.

Exhausted past all reason, she went upstairs to her own room while the pub still buzzed with its oddly relaxed energy and late diners.

At first she'd been relieved to be on a different floor than Aaron. Then, when she finally heard his uneven step climbing the staircase, she realized that his room was directly above hers. The old timbers creaked as he wandered back and forth through whatever his nightly ritual was.

It was a brief one. Once across the room, a shower so brief that she couldn't have properly wet her hair, never mind washed it. A brief silence that she suspected had to do with a towel, then a toothbrush. A few steps, then true silence.

The pub echoed with the silence. No rumble of traffic, like out her Charleston townhouse's window. No one downstairs. The silence of the closed pub in the small country town was so deep that it made her ears ring.

She could almost imagine hearing Aaron breathing.

Did he sleep in shorts or—

"Jane, you ignorant slut," she whispered softly, but it didn't stop her thinking about the "or" and how *her* stonemason must look sprawled on the bed wearing nothing but the night.

She'd been a long time going to sleep.

Now, in the morning, the sunlight shone into the pub's eastern windows. No locals by the fire, currently swept of ashes and rebuilt with fresh logs, but not lit. Only a few denizens were up and about—they must be the other residents of the B&B part of the pub.

A very self-absorbed French couple, elegant in form-fitting black, whispered intently together.

A round Welshman seemed to be regaling his equally round partner with a grand story filled with embellishments and many a sly word—none of which she could understand, but his Welsh rolled merrily about the room only to be crowded aside by his great belly laugh. It took her a few moments to realize that he was indeed speaking English rather than Welsh, but by the time she unraveled one word from its thick-accented cocoon, another dozen had rolled by. He offered something that might have been a "Good morning" but also could have been "Pork chops on Thursdays." Her tentative "Good morning" received a cheery smile, so she decided her first guess was more on point.

Aaron sat in the sunlight sipping tea and watching the world outside go by past the multi-paned bay window. In front of him was a half-finished breakfast.

She thought of going for a table of her own, but decided that was too chicken.

"May I join you?"

He startled as if she'd slapped him, almost losing his teacup. He waved a hand to the opposite seat.

Outside the window, a small village green separated the pub from the town's main road. There were benches that would be nice on a warm day, a few well-tamed shade trees. It was busy with people walking their dogs. Most were small, terriers and spaniels, but it had a different feel than Charleston, South Carolina. There were no tiny toy dogs. None of them had ornate leashes or little coats. These were simply village dogs out for their morning walk on canvas or leather leads.

On the narrow main road, monstrous trucks zipped almost carelessly past each other. Watching them, she could hardly comprehend her audacity last night of getting behind the wheel on an English road. And there was the earl's car, parked neatly in a spot that had opened close in front of the pub just as she was pulling up. Maybe she'd tell one of his people where it was and they could just come and take it away.

Beyond the road stood a jumbled line of village buildings. Most contained shops of one type or another. A bright-windowed tea room, sporting red geraniums above, occupied the ground floor of a building sagging with age. It was literally sagging. It had tilted askew in some bygone century. The ones to either side were centuries newer and stood straight and square, except the toy store and butcher's shop were oddly notched to accommodate the older building between them, as if holding up an old friend. An Indian restaurant occupied the next, a building so narrow it appeared to have been squeezed in between the butcher and the post office as an afterthought. The whole line was done in various ages of yellow limestone, their roofs varied between slate and tile. None had the charming thatch of her little cottage, where Aaron had been fixing her wall.

Aaron.

"Are you feeling better today?" How did he sense when she was thinking of him? Hopefully he hadn't been able to sense her thoughts last night.

"Was I feeling worse yesterday?" Yet she *was* feeling better.

"Hungover, probably jetlagged as well. You look..." he trailed off and studied his teacup for a long moment. "Better," he finally declared without looking up.

Bridget came by the table and offered her a plastic-covered menu. By the scuffs on the tough coating, the menu hadn't changed in a long time. She scanned it quickly.

A glance at Aaron's plate revealed the remains of scrambled eggs, potatoes, grilled tomatoes, sausage, bacon, and "brown" toast.

There was no sign of coffee on the menu, which was probably just as well. Jacking her system up for whatever morning crisis awaited her was no longer necessary. She was on holiday, perhaps permanent holiday. If so she'd...worry about that later.

"I'll have a bowl of fruit and yogurt with my tea."

Bridget stood waiting, her pencil poised.

"That will be enough, thank you."

Bridget's eyes widened. "Hal won't appreciate that. He includes a breakfast in the price because he expects folks to eat it."

"That's all I want, really." Jane could feel Aaron's smile, then could feel herself giving in to it. "Maybe a single piece of bacon. I like bacon."

Bridget spoke as she wrote, "Fruit and yoh-gurt. Bacon, one slice. You sure?"

"Tea."

Bridget rolled her eyes, but gave her a smile to go with it before walking away.

" 'Yoh-gurt'?" Jane asked Aaron because she didn't know if she actually had done something wrong or quite what was going on.

"Welcome to England. Here it isn't yogurt and café yohh-gurt and ca-fee, because we aren't in France so we don't go to a café. Toilet or loo, not restroom. Don't worry, you'll never figure it all out. And if you do, they'll just change the rules to mess with you."

Jane grimaced.

"You like following the rules, don't you?"

"I already got harassed for that by Bridget. You don't need to join in."

"But you *do* like your rules," Aaron didn't make it a question.

"Don't you have a wall to build?"

"On a Sunday? I'd be banned from decent society. Working on a Saturday was bad enough."

"Then why did you do it?"

And Aaron's eyes slid aside to watch out the window once more.

Before she could pursue it, Bridget arrived with her pot of tea. "Now the bag's just gone in. Let it steep some," and she was gone again. The teacup was thin porcelain and painted with her favorite flowers.

"Sweet peas. If England has sweet peas, I could definitely stay here."

"They do, though it's not the season yet. You're just in time for tulips and bluebells. Iris soon, too."

"How does a military man turned mason know about flowers?"

Aaron shrugged. "Grew up in the country. Helped Mom in the garden. She's partial to sweet peas as well."

"What's she like?"

Breakfast passed easily as they discussed families. She discovered that the pain of losing her mother and father had eased to merely awful. It was the first time she'd really spoken of them to anyone since the funeral and wake—an event Debbie had barely deigned to come home for.

Jane had had to use a major chunk of her own savings to buy half of their parents' house from her sister just so it didn't become some long, drawn-out issue. Jane only felt a little pinch that the ultimate sale price had been well above the appraised value, making her a tidy profit on the deal. The pinch was especially small now that Debbie had married into wealth.

Yoh-gurt and fruit had led to bacon. The yogurt was thick and Greek, the bacon was mostly meat rather than American that was mostly fat. She missed the heavy bacony flavor, but could get used to the more subtle English version. One cup of tea had led to four before the pot was drained.

"If you don't build walls on a Sunday, what do you do?"

"I usually walked down to The Slaughters."

"You go watch them kill things?"

"If you're up for a walk, I'll show you."

Jane was starting to understand the danger of Aaron's smile. He often used it instead of words as if daring her to say no. Knowing what he was doing didn't make it any less effective.

"Two minutes," she retreated upstairs, then brushed her teeth enough to clear out the bacon while changing into walking shoes. A light jacket and she, checking her watch, was back in a minute forty-five.

"What are you smiling at?"

Aaron looked terribly amused. "You did warn me that your job was being efficient."

"I *am* very efficient," it was her main claim to fame. Some project managers were all about communication, and nothing else. Her specialty had always been about discovering the most efficient and effective process for any task.

"We'll see," and he led her out the door without explaining himself any further.

AARON WAS INTRIGUED by this third version of Jane. Though he'd been watching her all through breakfast, he didn't know quite what to make of her.

The tipsy beauty in the stunning dress, who had fit in at the manor as if she were the heiress herself, had been magnetic. Jane's thoughtless sophistication and poise had only made Debbie all the less so in comparison. He felt a little sympathy for Debbie, not too much, at having to grow up with such a shining example of womanhood for an older sister.

Then there was the runner—so sleek and wired she might have been some fantasy cyborg from the latest teen science-fiction flick. Charlize Theron in *Aeon Flux* but shining bright rather than dangerous black.

And now this third woman ambling beside him as he sought the footpath across the stream near Bowl Farm. Slender jeans, a blouse the same blue as her eyes that might have been silk or some other of those sleek fabrics, and a denim jacket that hadn't come from JC Penny's or even Macy's. But on her feet were very practical walking shoes rather than her fancy running sneakers.

Stylish, understated, and she made him feel like a complete slob.

She started at a brisk pace, but he knew that wouldn't last.

Hoped it wouldn't. He could keep up, that wasn't the issue—his hip was fine now that he'd stopped fighting his body's new tendencies—and his knee was under control, with the help of a couple of ibuprofen. But at this rate she'd cover the ground awfully fast and he'd much prefer a lazy Sunday stroll. Plus she'd miss the subtle stuff. He had to call her back to notice a small patch of early bluebells tucked beneath a hazelnut grove. They came through a small wood, crossed an arched stone footbridge (mortared rather than dry-laid), and picked up the path, which turned south along a tree-lined lane.

That's when she slammed to a halt.

He did his best to hide his smile. He'd made a small bet with himself that Jane Tully was a total sucker for cute. It was nice to be proven right.

"Oh," she let out a happy sigh.

"Pretty damn sweet, huh?"

"As if you had anything to do with it."

Well, she certainly did a good job of keeping his ego in check. Though walking along with the prettiest woman in town wasn't hurting any.

The spring-green field in front of them was filled with white sheep. Big ewes, looking several times their actual size in thick fleece, were scattered all about the field. And every one was tended by one or two lambs. A newborn staggered to its feet while the mother watched closely. Another, perhaps only a day bigger, sprinted by. The newborn turned to watch it pass and fell back to the grass. A pair of lambs were locked in a fierce battle of king of the hill—their mother's back, while she lay chewing her cud, made the unobtainable pinnacle. A small gang of older lambs tested how far they dared get from their mothers, ranging out until the most chicken blatted out a "Mo-o-om." That call then caused the whole pack to call out and mothers to answer. Soon they were scattering back to wherever their mothers had wandered. Then, after a quick nurse, the most adventurous sallied forth again.

The queen of efficiency stood rapt, watching them so long that

Aaron almost wished he still wore a watch so that he could time her.

"This is why they invented the word bucolic," she finally said in an awed whisper.

"They actually forged the word in a smithy over in Naunton, I think," he gestured beyond the sheep pasture for effect.

"Forged it?" She turned to face him.

"I'm sure that's how they make words around here. Hammer, tongs, fire."

"You are so male."

"So you keep saying. Okay, Ms. Know-it-all, if they didn't forge the word in a Cotswold smithy, where did it come from?"

"Clearly, Mr. Smarty-pants, bucolic comes out of the Ancient Greek…"

Oh. She was one of *those* kind of people when it came to words.

"…for utterly charming. It was invented by a shepherd on a sunny, pastoral hillside on the island of Crete while wooing a baker's daughter who had brought him fresh-baked bread."

"Uh-huh." Okay, maybe his first judgement had been too harsh.

"You doubt me?"

"Don't know. Did he get the girl?"

"Of course he did. The sweet shepherd always gets the baker's comely daughter."

"I'll have to remember that." He hadn't really thought about "getting the girl" until this moment. He'd simply been glad of each moment his path had crossed Jane Tully's. What would it take to get a girl like her? What did that even mean? His relationships since high school were more easily measured in weeks than months.

"You aren't some sweet shepherd, Mr. Mason. So you can forget about that." She turned and continued down the trail.

Several lambs who'd been edging closer bleated in surprise and bounced away. "And no, you can't fake it."

Aaron would pay decent money to know how she did that mind-reading trick of hers.

~

"Uh-oh," Jane stumbled to a halt.

"What's wrong?" Aaron came up beside her and began scanning the field as if it was filled with snipers and tanks and things.

She couldn't imagine what the world must look like through his eyes.

After wandering through the back of a farm, in immaculate English countryside condition of course, and climbing a low ridge, they had crested the hill. A vista had opened out before them.

The fields and pastures, built with every color green in the world, were cut into neat sections by stone walls and well-trimmed hedgerows. Some of the sections were filled with the sunshine-yellow rapeseed, others with sheep and more lambs. A small wood traced the line of a stream along the valley's floor, leading to a small town of a few dozen limestone buildings and a stone church, all basking in the sunlight.

"What's wrong?" Aaron repeated, checking behind them now and up into the trees.

"What is it like to live in a world where everything is a threat?"

Aaron eyed her for a moment, scanned the countryside one last time, then offered one of his enigmatic shrugs. "Just like being careful," which wasn't an answer. "Now *what* is wrong?"

"I'm having a problem with the word bucolic."

His eyes crossed for a moment as he tried to make the mental shift from whatever military-attack scenario had been filling his head.

"Seriously," she waved at the view ahead. "If our first stop was 'bucolic,' then what am I supposed to call this?"

"Bloody bucolic?"

Jane liked how smoothly Aaron adapted to a changing situation. "But there's that B-word you were warning me about."

"Ruddy bucolic," he made it a declaration.

"Does it get nicer than this anywhere? This seems kind of pinnacle bucolic to me, but it's my first time in England." As if to prove her point, a trio of riders on horseback came up the trail behind them. They offered simple nods and a friendly, monotone "Morning!" before continuing ahead to become part of the landscape.

Aaron scratched at his nose for a moment, "There's a little town a few miles that way," he pointed over the hills. "Notgrove is one of the prettiest places I've ever been. In the other direction is Greater Tew. It's a little *too* perfect for my taste, but all of the houses are thatched or slate and the pub is a good one."

"So if this is ruddy bucolic, there is at least one category above that."

He began leading her down the trail toward the little town. "At least two."

"Bucolic, ruddy bucolic, bloody bucolic, and if we're to be crassly American, effing bucolic."

"On the other end of the scale you could have BWR."

"BWR?" Jane trailed behind, appreciating the view. She remembered the bare broad shoulders of the man building her garden wall. Covering them in a plain black t-shirt only emphasized the line down to his waist. His limp worried her some, but it appeared to be less than it had been yesterday afternoon as they'd walked to the manor.

"Bucolic with restrictions. For when there's a cell tower or a highway in an otherwise bucolic setting. The big tower atop Icomb Hill," he waved to the south, "makes the whole area BWR."

Jane tried to think of any other man who had ever played such word games with her. *Against* her, sure. Larry the jailbait-hunting professor had been the master of that. For him, words were weapons. For her Vermont country boy turned stonemason, they were a game.

Forged in a smithy.

She *loved* that image. It was entirely too easy to picture a shirtless Aaron as the brawny blacksmith, sweating in the heat and slamming his fisted hammer onto hard iron as he forged out steel words.

Oh, Jane was going to have a hard time shedding that particular image.

At the hedgerow there was a gate. They'd passed through several different types already, including a simple flat board sticking through both sides so that it was easy to step up and over the fence.

This gate was made of two pieces. To one side, the wooden fence split into a narrow V. To the other was the gate itself, built so that it could be swung from one point of the V to the other. The trick was to enter the V one at a time, swing the gate over to the side of the V just used, and exit out the other side. Sheep couldn't make the turn, but humans could.

"How many kinds of gates are there?" She stepped in and swung the gate across the path to open her way out.

"Dozens, maybe hundreds, though there are only a few main types," Aaron rested his hand on the gate close by hers from the opposite side. "This one is called a kissing gate."

She stopped, suddenly aware of how close together they were and how far away from anyone else. Nobody here but sheep. Back home she'd never let herself get in such a situation with an unknown man. But with Aaron she felt no threat, nor did she feel particularly safer for his presence. Somehow danger simply wasn't relevant here in the Cotswold sunshine.

Instead she was feeling…happy. Which was actually a little unnerving.

"The bucolic must be going to my head," she whispered as he watched her with those steady, all-seeing eyes of his.

"Why is that?"

She thought that the two of them standing in a kissing gate made that rather obvious, but if she needed to explain it more clearly, she didn't mind.

This time she wasn't drunk or exhausted when she leaned forward to kiss him. Perhaps she'd meant it as a small peck, a token to acknowledge their passage through a kissing gate. Perhaps.

She saw no real point in analyzing her true motives as she leaned into the kiss, holding on to the old wood with both hands to keep herself steady.

Aaron did the same, not reaching for her. Instead, they touched only at their lips and tongues.

The juxtaposition of this kiss to the ones that had existed so vaguely in her memory they were almost forgotten, brought both of those back to life. A hard kiss on a stone wall. A hasty one with his powerful hands sliding across her bare skin in his room that same night.

And this.

As warm as sunshine, as soft as the sweet smell of spring on the air.

He finally eased back, watching her, waiting to see what her reaction would be.

"How many of these gates are there around the Cotswolds?" She brushed her lips lightly once more over his and then stepped the rest of the way out of the gate. As she continued down the path, she didn't hear him following. A glance back revealed him still standing in the gate, not yet crossed over.

She could really get to enjoy this.

～

AARON KNEW SOMETHING HAD CHANGED. Something big. But he couldn't seem to wrap his mind around it.

How many of these gates are there around the Cotswolds?

Good god! If each got him another kiss like that one, he'd lead her to every single one and die a happy man. Being kissed by Jane Tully was—

She'd kissed him.

Not playfully.

Not drunk.

Stone cold sober in the broad light of day, she had kissed him. Despite the way he'd treated her yesterday.

It—didn't make sense.

Not that he was complaining, but—

"Are you going to stand there all day?" Jane called from farther down the track. "I've already kissed you at that gate."

Aaron got his feet moving.

First, he was *not* going to tell her that it was called a kissing gate because the gate just "kissed" either side of the V-shaped fence end.

Second, he needed to find another one, fast.

CHAPTER 6

"I don't know the last time I've had such a lovely day," Jane told their unlikely dinner companion Conrad, the Earl of Evenston. She and Aaron had just returned from their walk when the earl happened into the pub and joined them. She wasn't sure how to behave when dining with an English lord in a rustic pub, but his innate ease and graciousness made it easier to relax...eventually.

"I'm so glad," the earl sipped his beer. "The walk to The Slaughters is one of my favorites. I make it often myself."

The Slaughters had turned out to be two lovely little towns, Upper and Lower Slaughter. Lower Slaughter, straddling the River Eye (a grand word for a lazy stream less than twenty feet wide) had been especially captivating. She and Aaron had shared a late morning teatime in back of the Old Mill, watching ducks paddle about the mill pond that spread out beneath the willow trees.

"I find it so hard to believe what exists just out your back door around here."

"Yes, almost every direction will lead you into our trail system. There are several groups that lead rambles in the area. You can find ornithological, naturalist, and even architectural tour guides for walks that vary from leisurely ambles to the next pub, to long tramps along the Cotswold Way. There are even dog-walking groups."

"Like Snoop?" The dog was in his usual place by the fire. He looked up at her when he heard his name. She leaned down to give him a scratch.

"Don't know that old Snoop ambles much farther than his food bowl unless he has to."

He *was* a rather round spaniel—not as wide as he was long, but clearly working on it.

She'd ordered steak-and-ale pie and had decided that she'd never eat anything else here because it was so good. That was before she tasted the earl's sirloin steak that had apparently come from the earl's own cattle. She was definitely going to eat *that* next time; it was one of the best steaks she'd ever had.

Aaron was having one of Hal's Sunday-only roast dinners: a massive plate of pork, mashed potatoes, and veggies. The sharp malt vinegar of the brown sauce that he added tickled her nose. His right leg was propped on a chair. It worried her, but it didn't appear to concern him in the slightest. Toward the end of the walk he had grown silent, clenching his jaw. She'd slipped her hand through his arm but he'd shaken her off.

When she'd asked if he was okay, she'd received a sharp, "Fine." Then he'd sighed. "Docs say exercise is good for it. Strengthens it. I'm fine." Then he'd told her the meaning of the town's name as if to distract himself as much as her during the last climb up the hill to Fosse-on-the-Wold. "Fosse Way was the main Roman road through the area, almost four hundred kilometers in a straight line. Wold means 'upland' or 'hill.' So we're now approaching the town of Roman-Road-on-the-Hill."

Roman. As in two thousand years ago. Everything around here was old, most of it older than the discovery of America.

"Did you know my cottage dates back to the Civil War? Your Civil War," she turned to the earl, "in the 1600s?"

"You have a cottage?" The earl's question was no more than mild curiosity.

Aaron's beer was frozen in midair halfway back to the table.

"I made an offer on one."

Aaron's beer still didn't move.

"It's a lovely little spot called The Springs." She plucked the beer out of Aaron's hand and set it on the table before he dropped it. "What's your problem?"

"You are a woman full of surprises."

That didn't sound like any Jane Tully she knew. "Is that a good thing or a bad thing?"

"Careful there, Aaron," the earl was smiling over his Donnington bitter, but his tone was warning.

Aaron inspected the earl for a moment with a puzzled expression, then he turned back to study her.

Jane wanted to squirm in her seat.

"You startle me every moment of the day."

"Evasion."

"Good thing," Aaron finally declared and Jane felt as if she could breathe again.

How could she doubt that she was anything but good? Only the earl's warning had stopped him from blurting out that she was incredible—though he didn't think that was what the earl had been warning him of.

Like Trent's warning yesterday to "watch his line." It had taken Aaron until the middle of the night last night to figure that one out—for all the good it hadn't done him. Trent hadn't been referring to the line of the wall at all. He'd been referring to how close Aaron was coming to losing Jane.

Losing her?

He didn't *have* her. Someone like him *couldn't*.

But he also couldn't understand what she'd just done either.

Her life was a wreck. Her business and home gone. Her career blown up. Her bitchy sister married and giving her the cold snub.

And Jane Tully's response?

Be so strong that she bought a cottage in the Cotswolds.

Amazing!

And he could absolutely see her in the place. Not the manor-house beauty or the magazine-ad runner. But the woman who smiled at lambs and had teased him at every successive kissing gate with a peck on the nose or cheek. The one time he'd reached for her, she'd pushed his hand aside.

They're called kissing gates, not hugging gates. She hadn't been teasing so much as being…fun. He tried to remember the last time he'd had fun. Aaron had always *enjoyed* Delta Force training, but it was more likely to be called brutal than fun.

He wasn't sure which of them he was testing when he reached across the table for her hand and gave it a squeeze.

"Crazy good thing!" He told her.

Earl Conrad nodded his approval.

"Crazy. I'll grant that much," she started to pull her hand back.

Aaron clamped down on her fingers before she could wholly escape to make sure he had her attention. "No, I mean what I said."

"You always do, don't you?"

"I try."

"I'm learning to read your shrugs, Aaron Mason. What are you uncomfortable about now?"

"You've been mind reading my shrugs?" He wasn't even aware he had shrugged. Her hand escaped during his momentary surprise.

"That's why your evasive tactics don't work on me," Jane's

laugh teased him. "Besides, I'm not the only one doing the mind reading here."

She hadn't missed his evasions even once. He couldn't seem to get away with anything without her calling him on it. He tried to control his shoulders, but suddenly became so self-conscious that he couldn't decide what to do with them.

Jane's laugh said that she could see even that.

"Evening, Conrad." Hal had come out from behind the bar—tonight's sea-blue tie was cluttered with dozens of tiny sailboats apparently all racing for his throat. Snoop perked right up. Hal swept him up into the crook of his arm without even looking. The dog sighed happily and rested his head on Hal's shoulder.

The earl greeted him just as amiably. Over the three months he'd been here, Aaron didn't recall the earl coming in. Of course Aaron had only met the earl two days ago so he might have been in a dozen times without Aaron noticing.

Two days ago.

He eyed Jane as she slid effortlessly into their conversation, talking about the walk to the Slaughters.

He'd only met her two days ago.

Two weeks, maybe. Two months even. Two days? It simply didn't register.

"Aaron has an affinity for kissing gates," Jane revealed and earned a deep chuckle from Hal.

"Must say Bridget does as well."

So they *were* a couple despite Bridget's teasing. It still wasn't clear if they were a May-September couple or Bridget simply looked amazing for her age. How had it taken him three months to learn that?

People just opened up around Jane. He'd certainly revealed more of his past to her in two days than even to Trent in three months of working side by side.

There was a warmth to her, deeper and richer than the crackling fire that invited people in.

~

"I WAS JUST WATCHING THE LAMBCAM."

Hal and Snoop were so cute together Jane could just melt.

"What's a lambcam?" Aaron asked which saved her from feeling completely clueless.

In answer, Hal held out a tablet computer for her to see. On screen was a streaming video of the inside of a barn. It took her a few moments to make sense of the picture. It was a well-lit area spread with straw and divided into sections with steel fencing. Several sheep were standing near a feeder that must be filled with hay by the way they were pulling at it. Lambs scooted about the enclosure with varying degrees of confidence. From what she'd observed on today's walk, these were all newborns, probably less than a day or two old.

"What's wrong with her?" Jane pointed to the lower left of the screen. Even in the fields she'd never seen a sheep lying on her side before.

"Lady has a good eye," Conrad addressed Hal.

"She has two good eyes," Aaron seemed offended as if they'd been slighting one or the other of her eyes. "But that sheep does look like it's in trouble."

The screen flickered and a different lambing barn was revealed. This other barn was smaller and darker than the first, but there was enough light to see that all the sheep were up and about and all the lambs doing well. One staggering uncertainly to its feet was being licked clean by its mother.

"Those are Henry Wallis' sheep," Hal informed her. "He lives over the other side of Fosse. We set up a couple dozen cameras and fed them here so that the lads could feel comfortable leaving their sheds for long enough to fetch a pint of rest."

"Is that what you call it?" Aaron tipped back his half-empty glass for another swallow. "How about a stone wall cam?"

"Could do, but stone walls don't build themselves. Sheep

generally get through just fine on their own."

Jane could see the two men enjoying the sparring back and forth, but the lying down sheep worried her. "But what about the earl's sheep?"

He rose to his feet, wiping his mouth with a napkin. "I suppose I shall have to forego Bridget's dark chocolate-treacle pudding, which is perhaps a good thing," he patted his flat stomach.

"Don't you have a shepherd?" Even after only last night's dinner here, Jane had reason to know the dangers of Bridget's desserts. But today's long walk should be enough to balance it out. Besides, she was on vacation, wasn't she? Sort of a permanent one? *Grim.*

"I do have a sheep manager, but there's a fair number of birthing ewes and the man needs his rest. You're welcome to come along if you like, Jane. Your sister is well clear of the manor house. Aaron?"

At the earl's question, which sounded almost like a command in his cultured tone, Aaron looked up in surprise, then offered one of his *why-not* shrugs.

In minutes they were walking together down the footpath out of Fosse-on-the-Wold toward the manor. The last of the day's light and the presence of the two men accompanying her made it a warm and welcoming walk.

How different from when she and Aaron had walked this same path for the first time at this same time of day. Her terrible dread of the horrid wedding had lain in wait at the end and her drunken bravery had barely been sufficient to enlist the aid of a total stranger.

A total stranger who she now knew had an integrity as deep and lasting as the Cotswold hills, had shoulders she would love a chance to trace her hands down, and a kiss that sizzled even in memory.

Yesterday she had bought a cottage.

Today she was clearly losing her mind completely.

~

AARON SAT on a bale of straw with a newborn lamb in his lap and watched Jane, who sat cross-legged on the straw nursing another from a bottle.

It had been a hard birth and the earl still didn't have the ewe back on her feet yet. Instead, he'd set them both up with bottles to nurse the twins. Aaron had seen them in the field, but he hadn't realized what a scant handful a newborn lamb was. It lay neatly curled up in the cradle of his forearm, eagerly nursing on the bottle.

The lambing shed had gone quiet with the setting sun. There were just ten sheep in the comfortable space—only the ones who might need extra help were brought in here. Most had a lamb or two asleep close beside them. The only sound was the mother's heavy breathing and the suckling noises from two newborns.

Jane looked up from her lamb, now curled up in her lap and going to sleep. Her smile was utterly radiant.

How did she keep getting more beautiful every time he looked at her?

"It really puts me in my place," Jane pet the sleeping lamb as if it was made of glass.

"How so?" His own lamb was done but was struggling to stand. After the third time the little boy rammed a sharp hoof into his gut, Aaron set him down on the straw and watched as he struggled to his feet. Less than an hour old, but his instincts knew what he had to do to survive. Stand!

"It reminds me of what is important. My job always seemed so critical: *Get it done! Hit the deadline! Stay under budget!*" Jane blew a raspberry noise that startled the struggling lamb enough to make him fall back to the straw.

Again the lamb staked out his tiny legs like support struts to the sides and started upward again. His legs vibrated with the effort like a helicopter with one rotor blade shot off—impossibly hard shaking just moments before the crash.

He could feel it himself. The shaking in his arms as he struggled to support his full weight on the rehab parallel bars, his leg too weak to take the pressure of even its own withered mass from three more operations and a month flat on his back.

Just past halfway, the lamb collapsed back to the straw.

Like a good soldier, he barely waited to catch his breath before struggling upward again. Aaron wanted to help it, scoop a hand under its tiny ribcage and help it aloft. But he had to find his own feet.

Slowly, painfully, inch by hard-won inch, his lamb made it aloft. His four splayed-out legs barely able to support him. He simply stood there, vibrating with the effort, then he tried to pull one leg in closer. The pressure on the other three was too much and he sat abruptly, but the forelegs were still stiff and straight.

The lamb began again and Aaron mentally urged him to stay strong, to make it this time.

"Is that what it was like for you?" Jane's soft question snapped his attention away from the lamb. Her green eyes inspected him closely, able to see things even he didn't know.

"Hard work. A lot of strain and sweat. Yeah, it was like that," Aaron tried to look away but she didn't let him.

"He's whole, just weak. I'm guessing he has it easier than you did."

Aaron could only stare. How could she know so much about him? Delta Selection—along with its ninety-five percent failure rate—was a cakewalk compared to physical rehab on his rebuilt leg. Black ops, staring straight into the eyes of Death himself, was nothing compared to facing a mirror and seeing the man he'd become.

Jane didn't only see, she understood. It shouldn't be possible, but she did.

While he was looking away, his lamb not only found his feet

but managed several staggering steps toward Jane. He fell once, but was getting the hang of standing up again. When he reached her, he leaned his head into her lap and nipped his sister on the butt.

She woke, twisted, flailed, and tumbled out of Jane's lap before Jane could react. Her lamb lay on the straw blinking herself awake, then started her own trial-and-error experiment on how to stand.

Jane helped her lamb up, easing each hoof inward until the tiny thing stood almost four-square on only her second effort. Jane caught her when she fell, mothering the lamb beyond what any sheep would or could do.

It was so easy to see what kind of person she was and what kind of parent she would be.

God help him, but he was completely gone on Jane Tully.

Could he win her? Despite being some sad-sack, gimped-up—

He slammed the Black Demon aside before it had a chance to take root. He knew he didn't have a chance with someone like her, not a long-term chance. But he also knew that he'd never forgive himself if he didn't at least try.

JANE LAY IN BED, listening to the silence of Aaron Mason sleeping in the room above hers.

Cottage, stone wall, lamb birthing all swirled about her. She'd never forget any of it, but if there was one thing she'd never forget about today, it was walking back from the lambing shed in the quiet dark with Aaron.

He hadn't offered his arm as her White Knight was supposed to.

Instead he'd offered his hand and she'd taken it.

It was as if she had to learn about a whole new person. The tension in his arm was no longer her guide to his shifting moods.

Instead, she could feel every callus. Places where the rock must rub as it was lifted and placed. Or were they old calluses from when he was a soldier? Even Aaron's fingers were well-muscled. It made sense, but she could actually feel them flexing where their fingers interlaced. As intimate as any palm reading, every little shift filled with meaning she didn't know how to interpret.

Yet he hadn't spoken a word.

Instead, he had held her hand until they reached the stairs up to the rooms. The pub was dark and silent, everyone gone including Hal and Bridget. The fire was just banked coals behind a wire screen, offering the last ruddy glow as if the final bit of the sunset had been saved just for them.

At the base of the stairs, he'd asked a silent question with the turn of a wrist.

In answer, she'd faced him and slid into his arms. It was everything a kissing gate wasn't. His hard body pressed against hers in all the right places. When he scooped a hand up into her hair, it was to guide her head to rest on his shoulder.

All he did was hold her. He went so very still it was almost as if she was alone, if they hadn't been so close.

Was that what it was like to be with a good man? To feel...safe? Protected?

The feeling had become so strong that she'd finally had to step away before it overwhelmed her. All the Larry Jenkinses in her life had never prepared her for the power of an Aaron Mason.

I will defend her against anyone wishing her harm. Anyone.

She beat her head back against her pillow. Even in the fairy tales, White Knights didn't spout such lines. Yet Aaron had. And there was no doubt he'd meant it.

That's back when he thought I was a pretty blonde with an IQ greater than a gerbil and had my shit together.

Yet as they'd sat there earlier in the night, with the lambs struggling to stand and achieving the goal of being stable at about the same time as their mother did, he'd asked softly of her past.

It had spilled out.

The loss, the hurt, the pain.

She'd left out her fears for the future. Not because she didn't think Aaron would take them in stride as he did everything else, including his own handicap, she knew he would. Jane left out the future fears because she wasn't sure if *she* was ready to face them.

And then he'd offered his hand and his surety that somehow he'd decided she was worth it despite the mortal mess that was her life. He didn't promise that the future was going to be okay, but she could see the possibility whenever he was around…even with him sleeping on a separate floor above her.

She thought about tiptoeing up the stairs and sliding quietly into his bed so that he'd find her there when he awoke. Just another of Jane's silly fantasies. He might welcome her, but why would he want her? If he really knew her, he wouldn't.

The other problem was that she couldn't read between his lines on this. A shrug could only convey a certain layer of information. If he wanted her, why didn't he do something about it? At least kiss her at the bottom of the stairs. Maybe his knee wasn't the only thing shot up in the war. That didn't fit either or he wouldn't have kissed her the way he already had on their walks. But tonight he'd simply cradled her head upon his shoulder long enough for her speeding heart rate to slow, then wished her goodnight.

It was impossible to imagine his confidence was what had been taken down by enemy fire. Aaron Mason was the most competent man she'd ever met. Nothing seemed beyond him— from building rock walls to birthing sheep, to fitting into this very close community of Fosse-on-the-Wold. She'd have been a complete outsider if not for the doors he opened with the locals by the simple act of being seen with her.

She didn't know what to think of him, but the knowledge that her White Knight was there, just one room away, finally let her slide into unconsciousness.

CHAPTER 7

For days Aaron had done what he'd always done: gotten up, gone to build stone walls with Trent, had a slow dinner at the pub, and gone to bed.

But for all the similarities, his comfortable, well-worn routine hadn't been routine at all. When Jane had discovered what time he always had breakfast, she'd adjusted her schedule so that she could join him. Each evening they shared dinner.

One night they'd gone out to The Indian Princess and split chicken jaipuri and garlic nan for a change of pace. It was the first time he hadn't eaten in the pub in weeks. Even in casual Fosse-on-the-Wold, he'd felt underdressed as he sat at the white linen tablecloth across from Jane. Her taste was impeccable—the simple emerald blouse made her green eyes look warm rather than cool and the thin gold chain about her neck had made him want to trace his finger along its length where it dipped inside the open collar.

His decision that if she was willing to be around him, he was going to stop being an idiot by pushing her away was less helpful than he'd hoped. Flirting across a kissing gate and holding hands when they walked was a long way from his aching need to take her down every time he looked at her. He didn't care where: bed, floor, the side of some remote footpath among the bluebells. Didn't matter.

Yes, it had been a year now since the last time he'd bedded a woman, but that wasn't it—not all of it, anyway.

He wanted Jane Tully like he'd never wanted anyone.

By Friday morning as he headed over to work on the cottage, it had gone from exquisite torture to ridiculous. Each night, because the stairs were so steep and the landings so small, it was too awkward to steal a kiss, let alone embrace. The pub itself was busy later than usual so the base of the stairs was out. And if he led her out into the darkness of the night, self-control was going straight into the rubbish bin, which also wouldn't do. It had also been chilly and drizzling all week, which had taken the fun out of that idea.

Lying awake half of every night as he thought about her wasn't helping his attitude either.

Friday had dawned sunny and it shifted everyone's mood. Breakfast—which had included a lesbian couple down from Newcastle and a Chinese couple with no English and a co-traveling translator who wasn't much better—had a lively energy to it. Another major bonus today would be that when Jane Tully went running by the cottage, she wouldn't be swaddled in rain slicks. The spectacle of her running by was something he'd looked forward to every morning.

It was also nice to work on the wall out in the sunshine. But lunchtime was fast approaching and, though he'd kept an eye out, no sign of Jane.

"You keep craning your neck like that, you're liable to break it," Trent harassed him.

"Worth it," was Aaron's reply, because that was absolutely the truth.

Trent's lined face might have smiled.

Several hours later, Trent sat on the pile of rock and rolled a cigarette. "Making good progress." Trent actually sounded pleased, an event rare enough to make Aaron stop. He studied the wall. It ran for over a dozen meters in a great curving arc. It invited rather than excluded.

At least the property owner hadn't wanted to build a two-meter-high wall, plus the vertically-placed capstones. It was a classic Londoner thing: buy a cottage, then raise the wall height for "privacy." That had been Trent's grumble through the first week of tearing down the old, failing wall. "Londoners always trying to wall off the Cotswolds."

"Your lady buying the place?" Trent puffed away.

"Not my lady, but that's her plan."

"She the welcoming sort?"

"What the hell are you asking, old man? It's none of your goddamn business if she—"

"Wasn't asking if she took you to bed, though I can see now she hasn't. Was asking if she was the sociable or unsociable sort."

"Oh," Aaron decided that the less he spoke, the better off he'd be. He turned back to select stones for the next rise. "Self-contained, but sociable." He thought of her casual ease with the earl and the others at the pub.

"Reckon she'd like a gate in her wall?"

Aaron straightened slowly and surveyed the landscape. A complete wall would make the cottage very self-contained and cozy. A gate would open an access to the footpath that ran along the lower edge of the property. Without it, it would take a long sidetrack down the lane that ran on the other side of the cottage in order to reach the footpath.

"Yes," Aaron knew. "She'd like it." He'd seen how she lit up tramping over fields and paths.

But it was more than that. The way Jane Tully saw herself, she'd want to have the wall closed, keeping her safe and secure from a life that had hounded her into so many hard corners. Aaron knew her though, perhaps better than she did herself in some odd fashion. With a gate as a connection out into the wider world, it would give her permission to venture forth and become the startling woman he already knew her to be.

"Not placed front and center, but rather off to one side," he pointed to where the lower edge of the curved wall would eventually meet the wall along the property's edge. "She's partial to kissing gates."

Trent scoffed. "She's not planning on keeping sheep, is she? Can't fool me, I know just who is partial to those gates. My Elsie, rest her soul, made me right partial to them as well. No, this place wants a proper gate. About time you learned some arch work, lad."

Arch work? Making a dry-laid stone arch was a fearsome project. They were rare, though he'd inspected carefully the few he'd ever seen. Perhaps the pinnacle of an English master stonemason's craft. He doubted if there were thirty men alive who could build a proper and traditional mortarless arch. He hadn't thought about it, but it made sense that Trent was one of them. He'd also heard such knowledge was rigorously hoarded, so why was Trent willing to teach him, unless—

"Stop looking at me like that. I'll be kicking my clogs soon enough, but there's no need to rush me on the way. I'll teach you because I trust your eye and hand, not because I'm afeared that I'll die before I teach you."

Trent was right. He was one of those small, wiry sorts who would probably live to a hundred-and-twenty just for spite.

"It wants to sit down by the end of the wall. We'll start on it next week. Do it before we finish the rest of the main wall as we'll need to work it from both sides. Now you keep on, I've got to go up to ruddy Moreton." He said it as if it was a teeming metropolis a hundred miles away.

Moreton-in-Marsh was a bustling town of just four thousand people that lay all of five miles away. Stow-on-the-Wold was much closer—half the size and, because it didn't have a train station, also much quieter. Except during tourist season. He'd take the added remoteness of Fosse. Five hundred people, it had bus service on Thursdays only. Thankfully, it was a short walk over the fields to Stow on the rare occasions he needed the bus.

He liked it here—the English version of his childhood home in Jay, Vermont. Small, sleepy, out of the fray. For true locals, Moreton *was* "the big city" that was visited only reluctantly and he was starting to feel that way himself.

"I'm going to get you a t-shirt, old man," he picked up the next stone and waited for the question.

"All right, you daft skiver. What will this wonderful t-shirt say on it?" Trent ground to his feet and pulled on his jacket.

" 'Not Moreton! Again?' "

It earned him a sharp bark of laughter that did Aaron's soul good. Trent really did look ancient today and it worried him a bit.

Trent slapped his tweed cap against his thigh as if to beat some shape into the miserable old thing, snugged it on his head, and headed up the garden path.

JANE STOOD at the head of the path and watched Aaron working.

She'd passed Trent on the lane, who'd given her one of his welcoming grimaces. She couldn't tell if she amused or irritated the old mason. Were women not wanted on the jobsite where manly men did manly things? Maybe he thought they didn't belong where any work was being done at all. Perhaps it was something about her in particular? Or was he just an irascible old man who scowled, like a groundhog exposed too soon to the sunlight when all he really wanted to do was hibernate another six weeks? There might have been a smile behind it, though she couldn't make any sense of that either.

The view from the top of the garden path had stopped her. The opposite hillside was thick with ewes and lambs. The sun sparkled off the practically phosphorescent green of new leaves on the scattered trees. Patches of daffodils dotted the spring-green grass.

And once again Aaron had peeled his shirt off in the warm midday sunlight, definitely a plus to the view. He worked steadily and methodically, choosing and placing stone. He favored his knee, but he didn't let it stop him for a second either.

"Here is 'man,'" she said it softly. She'd accused him of being so male, but that had been no more than a pale shadow of the muscled ex-soldier building a stone wall in her front yard this morning.

Her front yard.

She clenched the key tightly in her hand, felt it cutting into her palm, and didn't care.

Hers.

Well, not really hers, but the owner had allowed her to rent it month-to-month while they were negotiating the final contract and she was arranging financing.

Her cottage.

It made her feel both giddy and slightly nauseous. She had a cottage, an English cottage, but no furniture. So she'd spent the morning running around getting only the very basics: a cooking pot, a can opener, a towel, and an air mattress with sheets and blankets. She'd never camped before, but she wanted to see just how little she actually needed. No condo with all the couches, chairs, and tables for entertaining—which she'd never had time to do. No need for a guest room that had never been occupied by more than dust.

It was time to simplify her life.

Her one luxury was awkwardly stuck upside down in the back seat of the earl's MINI Cooper. In a Stow-on-the-Wold thrift shop she'd found the perfect wing-backed armchair for the upstairs window, cheerfully covered in all the shades of spring.

Her last stop had been to purchase a bribe to elicit Aaron's aid in getting the chair where she wanted it to go.

And now in her front yard was Aaron Mason, right where she'd hoped to find him. But so much more of him than she'd expected to encounter. She wanted... Jane didn't know what.

He didn't hear her as she moved down the path. It offered her a splendid view of his back muscles rippling in the sunlight. Strong arms and hands selecting yellow rock from the pile with all the grace of a dancer. As if they selected the next stone without him.

"Morning," she had learned the slightly flat monotone that the locals used. She wondered if in different parts of the Cotswolds they used different notes or if the natives always used that same just-a-little-flat greeting with no sing-song at all.

Aaron dropped a stone, thankfully a small one, but didn't appear to notice as it bounced off his boot.

"There you are," he turned to face her, his smile huge.

"You were expecting me?" She'd thought to surprise him.

"I enjoy watching you run along Heart of England Way each morning."

She only had to arch an eyebrow to elicit a look of chagrin. Then he offered one of his *you caught me* shrugs.

"You're very easy on the eyes, Jane. Have to give a guy some latitude on that."

She wasn't so sure about that. "Guys" had always been more of a problem for her than any help. However, she found herself willing to give Aaron that latitude even though he was the most *guy* she'd ever met. The fact that she was now babbling made her thankful it was only inside her head.

Aaron made a show of inspecting her head to foot, then grinning like a lunatic.

"Heart of England Way?"

"Sure, that's your footpath there on the other side of the wall.

Runs about a hundred miles and connects to just about everything else."

"Really?" She'd seen signs, but never really paid attention. It was hard to lose track of Fosse since it was up on the hill, so she just ran wherever the path led her.

"Really. What's in the bag?"

"My house key."

He looked at her strangely, "Must be a pretty big key."

She inspected her hands. One definitely held her new house key; it was still cutting into her palm like she was clutching onto a lifeline. The other was a brown paper bag from the Chinese take-out—no, takeaway—just down the street from The Princess of India.

"Oh, lunch. I brought lunch. I hope you're hungry. I brought enough for three but I passed Trent on the lane. Does he always look that grouchy? Or is it just me? I thought the food might act as a bit of a bribe since I'm going to be living here and..." Now the babbling had moved outside and it took all of her willpower to squeeze it off to a slow trickle, and finally silence.

"I *am* hungry and he's headed off to Moreton. He hates Moreton. And if he hates you, then he hates me."

"How's that?"

"Because he keeps trying to push me in your direction."

"Is that a bad thing?" Why in the *world* had she asked such a question. *Just shut up, Jane!*

"Not from my point of view."

Jane tried to wrangle her jumpy nerves into some semblance of order, at least enough for her to think. Aaron wasn't complaining about Trent pushing him toward her. Which, unraveled, meant that he did want to be closer to her despite the unholy mess she was at the moment.

Thankfully, years of living with Debbie had trained her well. *Keep all emotion hidden behind a calm exterior.* If she didn't, her little sister would use it as a focus of full-on attack.

She was half amused as Aaron quickly built them a low rock table on the lawn and they sat down across it with all of the dignity of a king and queen. Or at least a king and queen who didn't mind getting slightly damp butts from the drying grass.

As she laid out the lunch, Aaron started to put on his t-shirt.

"What's that scar?" A jagged line the length of her hand angled upward across his ribs.

He stopped, which may have been the real point of her question (though she wasn't sure) as he had such a nice chest. "Knife fight in a bar."

"You were in a… That doesn't sound like you at all."

"Kandahar, Afghanistan. A cleared Afghani worker turned out to be Taliban and tried to slice a couple of us over cold sodas."

"I thought you said a bar."

"Dry country, so no alcohol on base—at least not legally. But it had everything else: loud country music, a floor that stuck to your boots, crappy food, a lumpy pool table with cues all warped by the heat. Everything a growing boy could want from a bar."

"Except for the guy with the knife."

"Except for him. And no beer."

"What happened to him?"

At her look, she was sorry she asked and focused on setting up the containers on the stone table.

He went back to tugging on his t-shirt.

"What about that scar?"

He gave up and flopped his t-shirt over his shoulder, then looked at the circular mark on the other side of his chest. "Libyan nutcase dumb enough to shoot me just because I was trying to kill him."

"And…" She wasn't sure what was wrong with her and why she so needed to know all of this. It seemed ghoulish. Like all those movie scenes, "show me your scars and I'll show you mine." Except hers consisted of the time Debbie had thrown a hammer at her, claws first, and the time she'd cut her foot on an old railroad tie while walking barefoot on one of the steel rails. Debbie had pushed her off, of course.

Aaron eyed the small scar she'd pointed to just above his right hip. "Now that one really sucked."

"Compared to being knifed and shot? What was worse than those?"

He left her hanging while he uncovered the containers and took his first forkful of oyster beef.

"What?"

"Terrible. I hate to even think about it," he shivered but his smile gave him away as he picked up a skewer of chicken satay.

"Oh. Appendectomy," she guessed and he confirmed it with a laugh. At least *something* about him was normal. "Couldn't you use your super-soldier powers to will it out of existence?"

"I was a kid of twenty-two, serving in the regular Army. What did I know about super-soldier powers?" Then his scowl turned bitter. "Sure lost those," he tossed the chicken back down.

How could he think so little of himself?

Easy, Jane. Just look in the mirror. Well, she'd gotten pretty sick of not thinking much of herself as well. Her year had been hell and Debbie's wedding had only capped that off. Enough already.

"Come here," she said softly.

"I am here," Aaron shrugged.

She leaned forward. "No, here."

He leaned in, still sulking.

"Closer."

His smug smile said he was sure that he was about to get a kiss. He was close enough she could feel his body heat and suddenly wished she'd let him put on his t-shirt. To smell the mixture of sweat, limestone, and earthy male that made her want to devour him. Well, the kiss had been Plan A, but she didn't want him to get too smug. Instead, she leaned to the side and whispered into his ear.

"Shut up and eat your goddamn chicken."

His burst of laughter made her ears ring, but also told her she'd made exactly the right choice. "You'd make a hell of a drill sergeant because that's totally Army thinking."

~

AND IT WAS.

Shut up and eat your goddamn chicken. Stop worrying about all the things that he couldn't do anything about. His knee was blown. All the physical therapy in the world wasn't going to get him back into Delta. Even a new knee wouldn't do it, there'd been too much muscle and tendon damage.

So sit beside the beautiful woman in an idyllic garden, shut up, and eat your goddamn chicken. In other words: move the hell on.

Somehow Jane Tully understood that.

"Who *are* you, lady? Because neither beautiful woman nor Faerie Queen begins to cover it." Besides, she was killing him in that light t-shirt and shorts. They ended mid-thigh, but still they showed that she had forever-long, runner-amazing legs.

"Faerie Queen?"

"Okay, should have kept that image to myself, but it fits."

"Especially because I have a fairy-tale cottage." She held out her hand, palm up, and unfolded it to reveal a house key she'd been clutching like a dirty secret. It caught the sunlight and glittered gold in her palm. He could see by the angry red lines how hard she'd been holding on to it.

Remember that, doofus. She's fighting a battle with her own crap too.

But he couldn't speak.

She'd been at the B&B less than a week and now she was moving out. He'd known her for seven days but he knew her better than any other woman all the way back to high-school Mary. And Jane knew more about him than…well, apparently even himself.

Eat your goddamn chicken and move the hell on. The perfect advice of a moment ago now roiled in his gut.

His thoughts were in turmoil, but he could see her waiting for a response.

"Already?" He managed, but knew it wasn't enough. "That's so fast. It's amazing."

"Thanks." Apparently he'd said the right thing. He'd been talking about the unwarranted speed of everything—faster than a crashing helo—but she took his words as congratulations and he wasn't about to correct her.

CHAPTER 8

"I'm not a weakfish," Jane protested. She'd never liked taking that from other men and she certainly wasn't going to take that from Aaron. She'd be damned if she was going to stand aside like some helpless female while he did the work himself.

"Right. Sorry. Lift in unison—on three."

She'd also never met a man who could shift his mental framework so agilely. It was also, she now knew from experience, a mistake he wouldn't make again.

On three, they lifted either side the upside-down armchair out of the MINI's back seat, flipped it over, and set it upright on the ground.

"Where does it go?"

"Third floor. And the stairs are as narrow as the ones at The Queen's Guard, maybe worse. Are you sure your leg will be okay with this?"

"Sure. It's strong, taking the weight isn't the problem. I forget to pay attention and twist it—that's when it stops being fun."

Despite her protest, there was no way she could move the chair herself, so she took him at his word, bent down, and lifted her side. With two people, it wasn't very heavy and they had it up the stairs in a matter of minutes.

"Wow!" Aaron's single soft comment when he turned his attention to her third-story aerie was all of the compliment she needed. "This room is so perfectly you."

Jane could only nod in wonder. If he thought that, then he truly saw her—despite all of his "beautiful woman" and "Faerie Queen" nonsense.

"Paint in a light yellow, maybe daffodil. A small desk of dark wood," she blurted out to cover her surprise.

He tapped the sloping ceiling toward the back of the room. "Put in a small gable here and you'd have a great view of the front garden, the lane, and the spring with its watering trough. It would also bring in some more light."

"That's a little out of my league."

He shrugged one of his *no-problem* shrugs. "Except for the thatch work, I could knock that in over a weekend if you want."

"I don't own it yet. I'm just renting the cottage for now, until we finalize the sale agreement. But I like the idea."

They toured downward through the cottage. It felt strange standing with him in the master bedroom. Thankfully, he quickly moved into the bath and began commenting on the tilework and fixtures. It was a small space, so she was glad of the excuse to stand out in the bedroom and merely look in.

"Where did you learn all this?"

"Last couple years of high school I worked as an assistant for the town's fix-anything guy. He hoped I'd take over the business and taught me everything from stone walls to renovating a bathroom. Dad's a farmer, so I grew up pretty handy as it was. There's always something broken on a dairy farm."

Aaron was thumping a finger along a stretch of wall as if he could read what was going on inside it.

"This section of plaster needs replacing. Depending on the

fixtures you want, you'll want to get some green board in here against the moisture. Needs a vent fan too, which is why you have the problem in the first place. Again easy, call it a weekend for the fixes and a week to replace the tile and fixtures. Maybe a little longer because the plumbing probably dates back to the Napoleonic wars."

He strolled back across the bedroom as if wholly unaffected by their proximity where her bed would eventually go. King size, she decided. The room was big enough. If Aaron could figure out how to get it up here, definitely king size.

If Aaron? She was totally losing it. Like they were playing house together.

She heard his feet thumping down the stairs and hurried to follow him.

IF HE DIDN'T GET out of that room fast, Aaron knew he was going to try and christen her bedroom right then and there. Wandering through the house was almost like touring Jane herself—the cottage was an intimate extension of her that was slowly wrapping itself around him, making it hard to breathe.

He could feel how she'd alter each room from her descriptions. She had a good eye for décor, at least it sounded that way to his untrained ear. To look at her, he'd have expected elegant or urban. Or perhaps matching antiques and period pieces. But as she described each room—simple, comfortable, cozy—it was like she was describing the inner woman who was dazzling him even more than the outer one.

What was worse was he could see what needed to be done to both update the aged cottage and bring it even more in line with her vision.

A kitchen able to serve generous meals? Rip out everything except the AGA stove, redo the small closet as a pantry.

The small den would become a cozy escape with a big couch, a small television, a decent library, and a refinished floor.

Remove the wall between dining and living rooms to open it into a single space. Maintenance of the stonework of the massive fireplace. Replace the crappy sliding doors with French doors leading out to the garden. It would be a showpiece of modern living in country style by the time she was done with it.

"It's all doable. Take a month or so of hard work, but none of it except taking out the one wall is even a real challenge."

He hadn't looked at her throughout the entire downstairs part of the tour. Only by focusing on what the cottage needed could he avoid how incredible she looked, standing here, in this place where she so belonged.

Where the hell do you belong, Aaron?

He waited.

Silence.

No answer at all. Yeah, that's about what he'd thought.

Fosse-on-the-Wold?

Jay, Vermont?

Back o' Bourke, Australia—their phrase for where the true Outback began?

It certainly wasn't here with this woman.

It took him two tries to open the damned sliding glass door some idiot had installed back in the 1970s. Go back to his wall. That's where he belonged. That he understood.

He had one foot out on the flagstone.

"Aaron?" Jane's voice was soft behind him.

There was just enough pleading in it that he twisted around to look at her.

Halfway there he knew it was mistake.

Too late! His body's momentum was already in play.

His bad knee let go. He struggled to compensate with his other leg, but there was a stone step down from the sliding door.

For half an instant he had the Wile E. Coyote feeling as he

stepped on air and found nothing there. Then he was falling—down and backward.

A glimpse of Jane's jaw dropping toward a shout of alarm.

The twist continued and pain slammed into him from his knee. He managed to turn far enough to catch himself with his hands moments before his face smacked into the rock path, but his bad leg kept going and he cracked his kneecap hard against the step he'd missed.

"Shit!" Aaron's shout of pain and frustration was hard enough to choke him with the dirt he blew off the rock. Trying to roll over, he fell off the garden path and into a flower bed. The way his luck was running, he was just surprised it wasn't full of thorny roses.

AARON HAD REFUSED both an ambulance and her offers to drive him to the hospital, but he did take two of the ibuprofen she kept in her purse. She considered offering him one of her emergency Valium (acquired specifically for dealing with Debbie the-sister-spawn-from-Hell and Larry the-jailed-jailbait-hunter Jenkins).

Aaron's protests that he'd "be fine in a minute" were completely belied by his one attempt to stand. He might be able to bear the pain, but she couldn't bear watching him go through it and had slid under his arm. Together they managed to get him sitting on the living room floor and she instantly regretted taking her one chair upstairs.

"Hold on." She rushed back to the car and brought in her other supplies for setting up temporary housekeeping, which included the air mattress.

Aaron was sitting there with his pants around his ankles, inspecting his knee, which was already twice the size of his good one. Thankfully he was a boxer shorts guy rather than a tighty-whitie type. Still, maybe *she* should be the one to take a Valium.

"Sorry, I didn't want to have to cut them off."

"Good thinking," she swallowed against a dry throat. A mug, she hadn't thought to buy a mug. She took her pot to the sink and filled it part way with cold water. After taking a long drink herself —she should dunk her head in it to cool down—she took it back to him. "Thirsty?"

"Uh, thanks." Aaron made no comment about her sole drinking vessel. The water dribbled around his mouth as he drank, that gave her an idea.

She took her towel to the sink and soaked half of it. Then she brought it back and wrapped it around his knee.

"You'd make a good field medic."

"Why? Because I can wrap a towel around your knee?"

"No. Because you take best advantage of whatever tools you have on hand: pot, towel. Out-of-the-box thinking. It's a good survival tool."

"Is that what you do? Survive?" She took her hands off the towel and sat back, more importantly, *away* from Aaron. She leaned against the raised stone hearth.

His *thinking* shrug said *maybe.*

"Is that really enough?" Jane knew she was asking for both of them.

"You trying to convince me that it's not?" Aaron shifted his knee, grunted, and eased it back to where it had been. Any sensible nurse would have known to use the blanket or one of the sheets to spread across his underwear-clad hips.

"I'm trying to convince *myself* that it's not enough to merely survive," and Jane wished she could do that. How many years had survival been all she was doing? Debbie, Larry, high-stress career? Alone? When Larry and eventually his clothes had gone out the door, it had been a relief. Now she was far less certain that mere survival still counted as the victory she'd thought it was.

Aaron scooted over to lean against the opposite wall. Thankfully, he grabbed one of the sheets and flipped it over his lap as he did so. They weren't that far apart. Until the wall came down, the living room would be close to the cramped end of cozy.

They sat in silence for a while.

For something else to look at, Jane inspected the room, started thinking about the house. Every one of Aaron's suggestions had pointed out a flaw in her "perfect" cottage. She could see them now, like broken bones. But he'd also told her what it would take to fix them even if she didn't understand half of what he said. Removing the wall he leaned against had included phrases like jacks, king studs, and LVLs (whatever they were). But he'd also offered time estimates on every project.

"Do you do all the big jobs first or fix up one room entirely, and move on?"

AARON TRIED to make sense of Jane's words. The ibuprofen was kicking in and—as long as he didn't move his knee—the pain was dropping away. Which led him to paying attention to other things, making the blanket across his lap the most essential element for his survival. Having Jane minister to him, kneeling so close that her hair brushed over his bare thigh, had definitely changed the direction of his thoughts. The distance across the living room wasn't nearly enough, but it was the best he could manage at the moment.

Think of something else.

Survival.

Were they both in the same goddamn rut? Wasn't that the ultimate joke—two separate paths to misery.

Well, being in a rut wasn't right for the Faerie Queen. And if a White Knight ever needed a good and worthy quest, it was to get her out of said rut. Besides, what the hell, maybe he'd find a way out for himself as well while he was at it.

"Big jobs?"

She pointed at the wall he was leaning on.

"Oh. That's not big, just a little messy mixed in with some careful planning. The kitchen is the biggest one." Even as he watched, he could see her orderly brain working things out.

"So you said there was about six weeks of projects here."

Was there? He walked mentally through the rooms again. That felt about right.

"That's what you said, anyway."

"Okay. I'll believe." Though he wasn't going to ask how she'd remembered and organized all of that—might make him feel even more inadequate than his knee already did.

"What if you had an untrained assistant?"

"You?"

"I can afford my own rates."

"But can you afford mine?" Could he afford his own? Working closely with Jane Tully for a six-week project was definitely going to test his white-knighthood to the limits.

Her eyes narrowed as she looked across the room.

"Crap! Okay, that came out wrong. I am *not* asking you to sleep with me to pay for my help."

"Then what are you asking?" Her voice was cool.

"The truth?" What was he asking for? "I'd help out just to be around you. Even just sitting with you in the pub makes me feel better than I have in a long time, Jane. I'm okay for money. I was raised working-class poor, so I banked pretty much every dollar for the last decade. Army paid all my living expenses. Even at apprentice rates with Trent, I'm still banking a third of what he pays me. I'd do the work just for the pleasure of your company. Besides, I like working with my hands. It would give me something to do evenings and weekends. Just feed me once in a while and I'll be happy."

Her lovely lips quirked up into an amused smile. "That may be the longest speech you've ever made."

He shrugged. "Talked more to you this week than I normally

do in a year. Twice that if you don't count the razzing that goes on within an action team."

"I could get to like you, Aaron Mason."

"I'm way past 'like,' Jane Tully." And he really, really had to go back to keeping his mouth shut. What came after like? Lust? No, that came before. He remembered the blonde beauty in the wedding dress as she strode so confidently into the pub—that was an image he'd never forget. So what came after like, but before… Crap! He definitely wasn't going there. Usually his head was pretty quiet, but she stirred things up.

Jane rolled to her knees and crawled across the living room. They were so close that it would have been too much trouble to stand for such a short distance. She stopped with her face just inches from his. Her green eyes were wide and as bright as the meadow waving in the breeze beyond the open cottage door.

"This…" she whispered and he could taste her spring-water fresh breath. "This has nothing to do with whether or not you help me on the cottage."

Then she leaned in the last few inches and kissed him.

IT WAS DIFFERENT. Jane hadn't expected that. After all, she'd kissed Aaron Mason any number of times, though mostly playfully over kissing gates.

If he had a crush on her, she was done fighting the crush she had on him.

She rested a hand in the center of his chest to keep herself steady. It was like pressing her palm to a rock wall made of powerful, living, breathing man.

His hand slid up, his fingers caressing the nape of her neck, his callused thumb stroking along her jawline. They were so close that his wrist braced against her shoulder as if she were leaning against a tree that would never let her fall.

And the kiss. Lord above! How could so strong a man kiss a woman so softly? It was a gentle, testing, welcoming, head-swirling, nervous-system-melting kiss that made her glad she was already kneeling.

His other hand slid onto her hip and guided her to straddle his lap.

"But your knee—" she could barely pull back enough to speak.

"Just don't kick it and we'll be fine."

So she was careful to raise her leg high until she was astraddle his thighs.

His hand slid down and she braced herself for the pain of the grab, which left her wholly unprepared for the power of his gentle caress. He brushed his big rough hand over her breast like a sculptor testing the surface of his finished creation.

She began to do the same.

He'd shaved this morning, but she could still feel it was afternoon. What would it be like to learn enough about him that she could tell the time of day just by brushing her palm over his cheek? She'd have laughed if what he was doing through her bra and blouse didn't elicit a moan instead.

His muscles felt as strong as they looked. Stronger. He had broad shoulders without being massive, but his strength ran bone deep. She'd never had a lover who was in such perfect condition.

A lover?

Yes, Jane. You're going to be lovers. And now that she'd finally thought that out loud, so to speak, she was fine with that. In fact, she didn't see much point in waiting.

Since he only wore boxers, his pants still around his ankles, it was easy to find the lower edge of Aaron's t-shirt and slide it off over his head. Across their little lunch table built of yellow limestone, his chest had looked beautiful. Now she went to peel off her own shirt so that she could see if his chest against hers felt beautiful as well.

Aaron was way ahead of her. Her shirt was open and her bra

loose when he tipped her back and took her into his mouth. The jolt knocked the breath right out of her body.

Even her best-ever orgasm had barely matched that flash of lightning.

Unable to catch her breath, all she could do was hold on. She wrapped her arms about his head and pulled him in hard, her body begging for more. And her White Knight delivered.

When he finally went to lay her down, she shook her head.

He stopped instantly and looked at her. His eyes were darker even than that first night in the pub, but he was waiting for…

"Oh god, no, Aaron. Don't you dare stop. But your knee." She couldn't believe he would even offer to stop at this point. It gave her a sense of control she'd never had with a lover. A sense of safety she'd never had at all.

She pushed lightly against his shoulder.

Without comment, he twisted aside from the wall he'd been leaning against and lay back on the floor as she still straddled him. No macho-male-must-be-on-top here. Was that a university professor thing? He was ex-Delta Force. She'd looked them up online and what little was posted about them said they were *the* most elite military force anywhere. So, she'd expected the most macho.

Not this one. Maybe because he didn't have to prove anything —he already was the best.

Still dressed from the waist down, together they rode upward, his hands on her hips, her breasts, her face, and back down. Everywhere he touched her was a caress, a suggestion, a plea until all she could do was give until her release slammed through her. An arching madness so far beyond pleasure that it was almost pain.

Jane. The same Jane who had always had the boring, mundane, steady-boyfriend lovers while Debbie'd had the hot, sexy types. Jane Tully had just found the embodiment of raw maleness.

And it was glorious.

She braced herself against that beautiful, scarred, masterpiece of a chest while the shudders raced through her. And when they eased and her arms wouldn't support her any longer, she lay down on Aaron's chest and finally learned that it felt even more wonderful than it looked.

~

"I WOULD PAY anything to see that again." Aaron had watched as Jane had shattered. As tears had streamed down her face without her even being aware. Of her mouth formed in an "Oh!" of surprise that her body could even feel what it had. And to know that he had done that for her.

"I'm not a peep show," she whispered somewhere in the vicinity of his ear—her voice still broken with rapid breathing.

"No," he slipped his arms around her bare back and marveled at how Jane felt both so slender and so substantial in the same moment. Unlike his battered hide, her skin was smoothly perfect and he'd never get enough of touching it. "You're a show-for-one kind of woman. No one could ever question that. I just can't believe that I'm the one who gets to watch."

She braced herself up on his chest, leaning on her forearms, and kissed him lightly.

Her hair streamed down on either side of his face and tickled his cheeks and ears. He used one hand to toy with the ends of it. He slid the other down under the shorts she still wore and cupped her against him. If she reacted that way partly clothed, what did she look like when—

"Aaron?"

"Uh-huh."

"You ever say anything like that again and I'll beat the shit out of you."

"Oh, okay." He'd thought it was a compliment. In the future

he'd keep it to himself how spectacular she looked when her release slammed through her.

"You damn well better believe you're the one who gets to watch."

"Huh!" He couldn't think of what else to say. Again, the ghost of Sad-sack Mason had extended its evil claws. Well, to hell with him. Lady said not to go there. He wouldn't go there.

If he really *was* the one who got to watch, there was another thing he'd *really* like to see.

"I would kill for a condom right about now."

"What else would you do for it?" And he could tell by her smile that this was definitely his lucky day.

"Anything! I'd…I'd…I'd install a new window in your private office."

"Uh-uh!" She waved the silvered packet she'd fished out of her purse at him as she shook her head. "Remember, sex has nothing to do with the renovation. We already agreed to that."

"We did," Aaron muddled around for a new idea as she crawled back across the floor to him. Somewhere in the fray, her shirt and bra had finally gone away completely and he was as mesmerized as he'd been that first night in the pub. She hadn't looked so incredible because of the amazing dress she'd been wearing. It was the other way around—the dress had looked so amazing because of the woman inside it. And now she was revealed in all her…well, in her waist-up glory. "I'll…wash windows for you."

"That, Mr. Mason, is a deal. I hate washing windows." So did he, but at the moment he didn't give a damn.

She stood briefly to strip off her shorts and panties. Perfection on Jane Tully didn't stop at her waist, that was for damn sure. Then she slid into an easy cross-legged position by his feet.

"What are you doing down there?" He propped himself up on his elbows to see what she was up to.

She didn't answer. Instead, she began untying his boots.

"Oh." He had a naked Faerie Queen taking off his boots, socks, and...pants.

Using only one leg, he raised his hips enough to shed his own underwear, but she got her hands there first and teased them down until he could feel his pulse in the one leg that was supporting his hips in the air.

"Oh my, Mr. Mason," she said as she finally slipped them free. "I think that we'll have to be properly introduced at a later time."

She ran a single fingertip down the length of him and it was almost too much.

"For now, however..." she sheathed him with only one more tease or two.

Jane finished crawling up his body until she could kiss him. Then, with a single smooth move, they slid together.

This time, when she peaked—when they peaked—she kept her eyes open and they watched each other.

"WE SHOULD DO this in every room in the cottage," Aaron held her like she was precious.

Another first Jane could get very used to.

They'd had cold Chinese food (she definitely needed a microwave) and managed to inflate the air mattress. Now they just watched the last of the sunset through the open door. The sheep and lambs on the far hill had quieted for the night. Birdsong faded. The soft scent of growing grass was all that invaded her new home.

"I think that's a splendid idea." But she didn't like the idea of it all happening too fast. Aaron hadn't happened too fast, not with how amazing he felt as she curled against him with her head on his shoulder.

"With or without the air mattress?"

She wanted this to last. Who knew where either of their lives were going, but she wanted it to last forever anyway. Or at least for longer than this weekend.

Their clasped hands rested together on his chest. She remembered holding hands with him as they'd walked back to the pub after the lambing. A man who liked to hold hands. She *definitely* wanted to stretch this out as long as she could.

"What if...we only make love in a room once it's finished. Once it's renovated and furnished. Until then, we only make love here."

"Bedroom is first," he practically barked it like an order.

She smothered her laugh against his chest because it sounded more likely a girly giggle of delight than a proper laugh.

"Your office is last," he declared just as definitely.

"Why is that?"

"Because I knew exactly what I wanted to do to you in that room the moment we set the chair there. Leaving your third floor office to last will keep me highly motivated."

The mental images that he created for her had heat rising to her cheeks and hope rising to her smile.

"Are you going to be able to work? Your knee, I mean."

"It's just a sprain. It means I have to put the knee brace back on, which I hate. And maybe do some of the physical therapy exercises, which I hate even more."

"You've been avoiding your PT exercises?"

"PT is Army for physical training. Being a civilian and doing PT for physical therapy feels like a joke."

"Would your knee have gone out if you'd been doing your PT?"

His silence was answer enough.

She freed her hand from his, balled it into a fist, and pounded the side of it against his chest.

"Hey!"

His grunt was satisfactory enough that she did it again.

"Ow!" He caught her fist in his hand, easily encasing it

completely inside his big hand as if hers had become embedded in one of his stone walls.

"No more skipping PT. Ever. You were a top soldier, now you're going to be an equally exceptional patient."

"Yes, ma'am." He didn't sound happy about it.

Her fist was still trapped inside his unyielding grip, so she moved her knee from over his hips to slide most of the way up between his legs.

"Yes, ma'am!" Aaron sounded much more respectful this time.

"Damn straight, soldier." They lay together in peace for a long time, watching until the last of the light had faded from the room and the sky.

"There's one other thing that I'll practice being exceptional at," his voice was little more than a whisper in the night.

No question what he meant.

Jane slid over on top of him. "You have my permission to practice that as much as you want."

He didn't answer with words.

CHAPTER 9

The financing was taking time and after a week, Jane sounded as if she was going to go mad.

Unable to wait—he was as impatient as Jane was—they began surreptitious repairs. That next Saturday, still wearing the goddamn knee brace, he tore apart the kitchen closet and rebuilt it as a proper pantry. It wasn't large enough for them to christen it properly, but they decided that—after shedding his toolbelt—up against the pantry door counted.

Jane stocked the shelves with food that told him they were both in trouble. His skill set included how to use the heater on a Meal Ready to Eat and not much more. She could cook pasta and dump jarred spaghetti sauce on it. A brief consultation with Bridget and he added a basic cookbook to the pantry shelf and a small gas grill to the front deck. The food became decidedly better, if not very exciting. He bought some spices and a bottle of brown sauce.

Any night they couldn't face their own food, they went back to the pub to eat. Sometimes the Earl of Evenston would be in— seemed it was a regular escape from his mansion—and they'd make a merry night of it. Though Aaron still stuck with "your lordship" rather than Conrad. His attempt at calling him the *Duke of Earl* after the '50s song Grandma used to play had fallen flat.

"Dukes are properly addressed as Your Grace. I'm not a Your Grace," the earl had used the driest of tones.

By the end of the second week, Jane contacted Harriet the estate agent who contacted the owner. He was apparently traveling abroad at the moment, but had "every confidence" that things would work out and gave them permission to go ahead with all interior renovations except the most major work.

Not wanting to overstep their bounds, they worked on the guest bedroom through most of the weekend. All it had really needed was some plaster patching and sanding, new electrical outlets, an eight-foot piece of trim, and a fresh coat of paint. He'd also had to spend a couple of hours getting the windows to open and shut properly.

The fresh paint smell was still too thick on Sunday evening, so they returned to the air mattress in the middle of the living room.

"Two weeks," Aaron settled his ear just over her heart and listened to the quick double-tap beat accelerate as he rested his hand over her other breast. He felt guilty every time he touched her with his rough hands, as if he would somehow mark her. But she leaned into it every time so he didn't feel *too* guilty.

"Two weeks what?" Her breath was a little short and her pulse rate was definitely up.

"Two weeks since the first time we had sex," he began working on the glorious task of teasing her body to life.

"Is that what we did?"

"Sure." Something in her tone should have told him he'd just entered dangerous waters, but he caught it too late.

"Aaron."

He just wanted to listen to her heart, cradle her breast, and breath in the wonder of her. Then sex.

"Aar-on!"

Distraction. He needed to stage a distraction until he figured this out. "Do you have any idea how amazing you look in a tool-belt?" And she did. Her hair back in a tight ponytail, plaster dust on her nose and cheeks around the filter mask he'd bought her. The shorts and tight t-shirt that were her choice of work clothes. She was an apt, if wholly inexperienced assistant.

"Not half as good as you, I'm sure." He heard a wistful softness slip into her tone. Getting back on track.

"But guys wear toolbelts all the time," he'd never understood what it was that always made women talk about guys with tool-belts. "It's not like it's anything special. But on you? Damned hot."

She toyed with his hair as he listened to her heart.

He let go of her breast and slid his hand down to trace the line of where her toolbelt had ridden low across those fine hips. "Very hot."

"You're going to have to do better than that if you want any tonight, soldier." It was her drill sergeant tone and he knew that there was no getting around it. *Crap!*

"Okay, what did I miss?"

"Sex is somehow crass. It makes me feel cheap."

He almost said that she would be the most expensive woman ever...but caught himself before he did because it sounded totally wrong. Even protesting that she wasn't cheap didn't sound right. He was getting a little better at thinking before speaking. But he didn't see the way out of it.

Her heart rate was slowing rather than accelerating. Not a good sign.

"Well, if it isn't sex..." he took a deep breath. "I'm not exactly comfortable with calling it something else." He took courage from the fact that she still hadn't stopped brushing her fingers through his hair.

She sighed. "Neither am I. But 'sex' still sounds cheap."

"Mutual pleasuring."

Her raspberry noise sounded very strange transmitted through her breastbone.

"Making happiness."

"That's good, but it should be about more than sex."

"How about if I just show you what I mean rather than trying to say it?" He slid his hand down from her waist.

"You know…"

He sighed and returned his hand to rest on her hip.

"We also haven't slept apart for a single night of those two weeks."

Aaron blinked in surprise. "We haven't! Is it a problem?"

"Not for me. You?"

He shook his head. It was strange though. He was used to relationships between deployments. Of course in Delta, being between deployments meant a shift from a state of brutal battles to a state of brutal training. Between long hikes, overnight scenarios, and all the rest, he hadn't spent every night in two straight weeks with a woman that he could recall. With Jane, it felt completely natural.

This time she let him distract her and he did his best to brush all of her questions away. Maybe even her ability to think.

Maybe even *his* ability to think. Because if this wasn't sex, were they "making love"?

WHY COULDN'T she say the words?

Her body shuddered to life. It amazed her each time Aaron achieved that Herculean task—she'd long since been convinced by former lovers that any problems with sex were all hers and not theirs until the belief was rooted deep inside her. And Aaron brushed that aside every time with such ease.

She arched against his palm and worried at it. If sex with Aaron *wasn't* making love, then what *was* it?

Jane decided that she didn't need to label it as she pulled him tight against her breast.

But—*oh, god, that was good*—she needed to understand it.

She recalled the long-suffering look in his eyes as he did his half hour of PT twice a day. It had pulled at her until she'd resurrected her old yoga routines and joined his workouts. It was funny. No matter how clumsy and out of training she was, he constantly lost count of his reps while watching her and had to start over.

Aaron was so...besotted with her. It felt as if she was lying somehow.

This isn't the real me, she wanted to shout.

"Please, god, don't stop," is what escaped on a hoarse whisper as he nuzzled the inside of her thigh with his soft tongue and an evening hint of whiskers.

If Aaron was "besotted," what was she?

Over the moon?

Besotted herself?

When he finally settled his mouth over her, all she knew was that no man had ever done what Aaron did. Not one man of her past had thought of her pleasure before his own.

Lucky.

That's what she was. As she bucked and writhed against him, dug her fingers into his hair to encourage him to do even more, luck was what she felt.

Maybe that was what came between "sex" and "making love." Between "like" and "love." The third L-word.

"Lucky," she managed on a gasp as he poised his body over hers before sliding into her and finally washing all the words away.

CHAPTER 10

"What are your plans today?" Aaron needed a distraction so that he didn't just tear the Lycra bodysuit off Jane and plunder all that he could.

He'd finally learned to keep count of his PT reps by matching her yoga counts. New exquisite position—admire it for a count of ten—then watch her lips silently counting each positional hold for twenty, thirty, whatever.

He was fast discovering that he didn't mind PT nearly as much as he thought he would. As a bonus, the knee brace had already gone back into the closet.

"I was going to patch and sand the main bedroom wall the way you showed me in the guest bedroom." Jane didn't reveal the least strain as she balanced on her belly and reached behind to grab her ankles for something called the bow. Her stretch raised her torso and knees off the floor until she formed a nearly perfect donut shape. He'd tried it and could only flop about like a drowning fish.

"Let's play hooky."

"Won't Trent mind?"

"No. It turns out the whole Moreton thing was about a wall

someone bashed in with a lorry because the trucker took a turn too tightly. That's why he's been so angry about having to work on it. *Should have lasted another century before I had to be touching it."* He'd been working on his Trent imitation.

It earned him enough of a laugh that Jane lost her bow.

"Fixing it up now means I don't have me an excuse to be living forever. I was right attached to that wall since I built it during the Roman Conquest," Aaron added an extra layer of grouch that had her giggling as she rolled onto her side to look up at him. He had thoughts of…but she started a series of sideways leg lifts and he matched his reps to her motion.

"What about the stone wall here at the cottage?"

"I'm told I have an in with the new owner."

"Maybe," she acknowledged with a smile. Then she rolled away from him and began her leg lifts on her other side. "But if you stop doing your exercises to admire my ass, you're going to lose that privilege."

Aaron started doing his squats, but continued admiring.

"Besides, I'm not the new owner yet."

"You will be," he didn't like the worry in her voice. "But we both need a day away. So let's just forget about it and play hooky."

"I never missed a day of school. Did you?" Up into a kneeling position to do arching backbends with her hair nearly sweeping the floor beyond her feet.

That was too much and he had to look away to keep any blood in his brain.

"I'm guessing by your silence the answer is, 'all too often'."

Fine. Let her think that. His aunt had been the high school principal. He'd never dared to miss a day, be any less than an A-student, or fail to letter in track and field *and* soccer. He stole a peek as Jane arched back again—the blood was not going to be returning to his brain any time soon. There wasn't even blood to his vocal cords.

"What's British for playing hooky?" Jane finally flopped back on the floor into "corpse pose," spread-eagled on her back. As if that was supposed to help him any.

"Skive. Skiving off," he managed as he finished his own workout.

"Oh, I like the sound of that. I won't play hooky, but I will 'skive off' for a day. You take the first shower."

Aaron staggered up the stairs and glared at the tiny, English-style shower. Definitely not big enough for two. As he stripped down, he rearranged the bathroom renovation in his head so that it would fit a bigger stall. Then he stepped in and set the water to dead cold.

Aaron said he'd drive.

Jane was going to protest, even though the English roads still freaked her out, until she saw him sitting in the driver's side. The sides of English cars might be switched, but the pedals were in the same order: gas to the right, clutch to the left, and the brake in the middle. So the work of the clutch was under his good leg.

After that, she decided to just let go of her worries.

Top down, hair back in a ponytail, sunglasses on: she *did* feel like the Faerie Queen being whisked away by her handsome knight in a bronze chariot. Or at least a Faerie *Princess*.

"Where are we off to, Sir Knight?"

"Breakfast." The car snarled happily as it climbed through the gears once they cleared Fosse and then Stow. The road up to Moreton she'd seen a dozen times. She realized with a start that was pretty much all she'd *seen* of the Cotswolds. Here she was living in a government-sanctioned AONB, Area of Natural Beauty, a future property owner of a historic cottage, and had seen almost none of the area. Just as they entered the all too familiar stretch of Moreton, Aaron turned aside, headed west out of town.

Within a half mile they were back in the rolling fields that never ceased to amaze her. But something was different. "Cows and calves. Where are the sheep?"

"Varies by where you are. They seem to clump together. Out toward Donnington it's horses. A lot of the big-race winners come from there. The earl is considered a bit of an upstart because he lives almost three miles to the south but is running with better than average success."

"Three miles? That doesn't make any sense."

"You've never lived in a small town before," Aaron didn't make it a question.

"How did you know?"

"Little towns always look so quiet to folks raised in cities. There's a massive undercurrent in them. Always things happening. Take this one, for instance."

The terrain changed abruptly as they plunged past a sign declaring they were entering Bourton-on-the-Hill. Suddenly they were climbing a steep road between two- and three-story buildings crowded so close to either side that it was barely wide enough for the MINI. Or so she thought until a red-and-tan bus descended toward them. Aaron squeezed tight enough against a stone wall that Jane could brush her fingers over the small clump of violets growing in a crack as the bus somehow slipped by with only an inch to spare. Her heart had burst and been left on the road, but Aaron didn't even blink.

"That pub there, the Horse and Groom," Aaron continued as if they hadn't just nearly been squished. "They win Pub of the Year in a local guidebook almost every year. A couple of very successful painters live here as well. You can bet that the locals know exactly where and wouldn't tell you if you got down on your knees and begged. Well, not me anyway. *You* might be able to magic it out of them. Small towns protect their own."

"It sounds nice."

"Sure, if you don't mind having no privacy."

"What do you mean?" With a final twist, they burst out of the high end of the town. She turned to look back and the whole town appeared to be that single, climbing street wide.

"How many people of the four hundred and fifty-eight in Fosse do you think are aware that we're practically living together?"

Practically living together. She hadn't done that since she'd thrown Larry Jenkins' clothes out the door after him. At the time, Jane had promised herself it would never happen again without a ring and a wedding.

Yet she and Aaron practically were. His toothbrush and a change of clothes had definitely already made the transition. Of course she'd planted a toothbrush as an outpost in his room at the pub as well, for the nights they didn't feel like walking home through the rain after dinner.

She swallowed hard, "Hal, Bridget, Trent, the earl, maybe the—"

"Everybody."

Jane waited for the joke as they descended briefly through a set of oaks, then began to climb again. Cattle had turned back into sheep on the other side of the wood as if transformed from one species to the other by magic rather than any farmer's plan. She wanted to go back and double-check if they were all standing in mirror image position to either side of Bourton Wood.

No signature-Aaron laugh appeared along with the sheep.

"Really?"

"Oh, some may not know our names yet, but they all know about the American couple who are shacking up in the cottage they're buying down Springs Lane. The butcher, the waiter at the Indian place, the news agent you bought stamps from, all of them. I've definitely gotten the evil eye a few times in the shops that I couldn't account for until I overheard that you're buying it on your own. Apparently I'm now a gold digger at best, a freeloader at worst."

"Who told them all that?"

"Welcome to a small town."

Through a narrow S-turn, bounded by ancient stone walls to either side that couldn't possibly let a bus through even without anyone trying to pass, they burst out into the open.

She felt dizzy, as if she was still twisting through the turns. With her parents gone, there wasn't anyone who cared about her personal life. Not a single person—except maybe Debbie, who would want to sabotage it for spite. Jane would get the polite questions from someone she was working with on a project, but it was with the comfortable assurance that all such details would be forgotten before her answer was even complete.

She wanted to deny it, but… Gwyneth the butcher had asked if *her man* was especially hungry when she bought her first roast—only to discover that she'd gotten one big enough to feed a family of ten (that took forever to cook). Buying shampoo, she'd been offered a second bottle of men's shampoo. At the—

"Everybody knows?" Jane still couldn't believe it.

"Uh-huh." Aaron slowed the car as one of the prettiest towns she'd seen other than Fosse-on-the-Wold came into view.

"This is Blockley." Aaron eased past a school and what she at first thought was a soccer field, but turned out to be a lawn-bowling green.

She could see that the town split here. They were entering it midway up the hill: newer buildings were ranged up the slope, the old town spread out down the hill below them. At a bus shelter that looked as ancient and stout in yellow limestone as the houses, he turned down toward the older section and parallel parked neatly despite it being the wrong side of the street. Aaron had all sorts of surprising skills.

"The *Aunt Dimity* cozy mysteries are set in a fictitious town that just happens to look exactly like Blockley, but there's a dirty secret," he leaned close and whispered the last.

"What?"

He came around the car, opened her door, and offered her a hand out. "The author is..." he looked up and down the street making sure they were unobserved, "...an American. Worse, she *lives* in the States. Utterly scandalous."

"Horrors," she agreed. Jane was starting to get the feel for this. "How could such a state of affairs be allowed to come to pass?"

"That," Aaron laughed as he led her down the hill, "is a topic of constant debate among the locals."

"It feels as if we're on a date," Jane sounded happy about it.

If buying a pastry and a pot of tea in the tiny cafe (that was also general store and post office), then going for a walk along High Street was all it took, Aaron was all for it. Actually, it did feel like a date, something he didn't have much experience with.

"I suppose that it is time we started dating," she double-squeezed his hand in one of her silent laughs.

"I'm trying to remember the last time I've been on one." Aaron really had to learn to think before speaking. It didn't count as a date when you bought a bar-babe a couple of drinks and went back to her place. There were always Spec Ops groupies around Fort Bragg trying to raise their score and it was hard to complain. But they didn't count as dates. "Been a while."

"Me too."

He hoped for her sake that it was for very different reasons. He knew he was shallow, but he hoped that he was the only one in this relationship who was *that* shallow.

"This is the main street?"

"Back when horses were cars."

"You mean the other way around."

He tried it both ways in his head and wasn't sure. At the moment he was thinking about a different kind of issue, and not very clearly.

Relationship?

From having awesome sex and helping her out on fixing up her house, they were suddenly *dating* and in a *relationship?* The world really needed to slow down for…a long freaking time, or there was no way he was going to catch up with it.

They strolled through the town. A few people waved from their gardens where the daffodils had departed but the tulips were gladly claiming reign. Winding rose bushes with stalks as big around as Jane's elegant arms were dusted green with new leaves just unfolding. Grass was rare, at least on the High Street side, as there was so little setback to the houses. There were occasional cars parked along the street, but little activity.

"Is it always this quiet?" Jane was looking up and down the empty street.

"It's a weekday. Most of the residents are probably in London working."

"That's so sad."

"But still it's beautiful."

She nodded, but he could see she wasn't happy about it. "Fosse is out of the way enough that its population is mostly permanent. It gives the town a different feel. That's one of the reasons I landed there after kicking around the area for a bit. That and Trent. I was limping my way through town carrying my life in a pack and there was this old bastard building a wall. I stopped to watch and before you knew it, he had me lifting and carrying stone."

"I came here for a wedding," she said it as if it was news he wouldn't know.

"Really? Anyone famous?"

"They wish!" And now the bitterness was back on top of the sad.

This was not trending the way a good date should be trending.

He hoped he had the solution for that as he turned down a tiny street called Brook Lane.

As they wandered down the narrow lane between stone walls protecting stone cottages, Jane kept trying to shake off her mood. After all, it didn't seem fair to Aaron. He was taking a day off to show her places, to just *be* with her, and she was being all Miss Let's-look-at-the-dark-side-of-everything.

Perhaps it was because the day was being so disorienting.

Without realizing it, she'd been "shacking up" with Aaron. There was no question how he felt about her body. Or she about his. He was like a drug her nervous system couldn't get enough of. They also got along really well. She truly enjoyed sharing meals and laughs with him. Working together on the cottage, she was learning new things every day, hard things she'd never been trained in. Each night she'd plunge into bed, exhausted, aching, and supercharged to tackle whatever came tomorrow. Each morning she woke close beside a handsome man who didn't put her down but instead, somehow, lifted her up.

Oddly enough, despite sleeping, eating, and working together, today felt as if it was the first time they'd done something together as a couple.

As a couple. In past relationships, the whole "couple" thing had been about going to a dinner party together or out to a movie or... It had never been about walking down a quiet lane on a day that couldn't make up its mind between a little too warm and a bit cool as big puffy clouds slid across the sun. One sprinkled about a dozen drops on them as it passed by, then the sun was drying them off seconds later.

At the bottom of the lane, the road turned to the right, and... went under water.

Aaron stopped and let her stare at it until she could figure it out. A small sidewalk ran along the street that was now under six inches of smoothly flowing stream.

"I...don't get it."

He pointed at the far end of the lane where the stream flowed out from under one of the oldest buildings she'd seen yet. For the hundred yards that separated them, the road seemed to be consistently the same depth underwater. A glance revealed his big smile.

"Stop enjoying yourself so much at my expense."

He ran a possessive hand down her back and over her butt.

"Cut it out, Aaron. Stop being so damn smug or you won't be enjoying *anything* at my expense." She twitched her hips aside so that his hand slid free.

He laughed and pulled her into a hug. "I feel better now. This had me totally stumped until I asked someone."

"Oh," she let herself relax into his embrace for a moment, then looked back at the strange underwater street. Not teasing her after all. Okay, not *only* teasing her.

"It's—"

"Wait. Let me try."

And unlike any male in her past, he actually waited and let her try.

"The stream is actually flowing through that building. I'm guessing it ran a wheel for a mill."

He nodded.

Mill house. Underwater street. The steep street they'd just walked down to one end of the watery lane. She could just make out another street coming down the hill in front of the millhouse.

"Horses. Horses with wagons. They'd come down one steep hill with loads of grain and have to climb back out the other with loads of flour. This let them cool off a little in the brook without unharnessing them." She could see the flow of the process and it fit, but that wasn't all of it. "I'm missing something. Why is the underwater part of the lane so long?"

"Damn but you *are* good at that. I bet you can see the horse and cart."

"Horses. That's a steep hill. I bet they harnessed them in teams."

Aaron surveyed the stream and nodded. "Could be. What you're missing is that the cart wheels were wooden. If they dried out too much, the wood weakened and the joints loosened. By running the carts down the submerged lane with every trip, they kept the cart wheels sound."

Jane stood watching the water of a bygone era. A simpler time when a process engineer could just be some smart person in a remote Cotswold village and make a change that counted. The solution was elegant on so many levels.

"Thank you, Aaron."

"For what?"

She bent down and took off her sneakers and socks. Then she rolled up her pant legs and stepped out into the stream. The water flowed smooth and cool over her feet and around her ankles up to mid-calf. The roadbed of small, rounded stones felt soft under her feet, worn smooth by centuries of flowing water.

Aaron followed her along the sidewalk, probably where the team's drover had walked with a lead, guiding the horses forward.

That's what Aaron was doing. Somehow he was guiding her back toward something, though she didn't know what. She let herself become lost in the flowing water. The cool shade from the line of cherry trees to the south, the last of their white blossoms fluttering down to slip by on the surface of the water. The line of pretty cottages lucky enough to spread across the hillside above the lane—the backyards of lawn and flower beds exposed, revealed only to those who wandered down this way.

A pheasant wandered through one of the gardens. Another one of her guides? Perhaps so.

"For what?" he asked again at the far end of the lane as she sat on a stone wall and pulled her sneakers back on.

She rose and took her time kissing him there, at that perfect spot where millhouse, lane, cottage, past, and present all came together in a smooth flow.

"For showing me why I did what I did for a living. No matter what went wrong with it, I loved the work. I loved understanding how to fit everything together. I'd forgotten that about myself. Thank you."

CHAPTER 11

The crowd on Dover's Hill roared with approval as the next pair of contestants stamped their way forward. The annual Roger Dover's Cotswold Olimpick Games on Dover's Hill outside of Chipping Campden had been in full swing when they arrived. Aaron had forgotten about them but some part of him must have remembered that today would be a good day for an outing.

For a *date.*

Jane's kiss had almost made him collapse into the flowing lane in Blockley and drift back to where they'd started before her transformation. She had walked in the water with the gentle grace of a deer browsing through the deep Vermont woods. Her steps had left almost no impression, as if she wasn't really there. No slogging and splashing for the Faerie Queen, instead she had flowed upstream in perfect harmony with the water, the sunlight, and the surroundings.

She had come out of her walk in the brook with her shoulders further back, her posture even more perfect, and a smile that really reached her eyes as if it was happening for the first time since he'd met her.

Transformed from merely incredible to outright stunning—as if she'd stepped into a different world.

Now they were in his world. Or what might have been, during a different era.

A great castle gate, complete with scaffold-built turrets and a rope portcullis painted black like iron, towered several stories high where it had been erected on the meadow. Knights in full armor rode about on massive horses. Footraces, hammer-throwing contests, food stalls, and general mayhem abounded. Lords, ladies, and tourists all flocked together in one happy crowd.

Dover's Hill itself defined the northernmost end of the Cotswolds. To one side, its high bluff offered a sweeping vista down over the vast, flat expanse of the Severn River Valley. To the other, the rolling hills were sliced by dark hedgerows and aged stone walls dividing the yellow rapeseed from the green meadows salted with white sheep.

The main event had drawn everyone into a grand circle before the castle gates. With a great trumpet fanfare (and only a few off-key notes) announcing: the World's Grandest Annual Shin-Kicking Contest Dating Back Before Time Was Time To the Glorious Reign Of When King James The First Set His Royal Backside Upon The English Throne!

The sport of shin-kicking was simple and insane—Delta Force-style insane.

The first two combatants grabbed each other's shoulders. After another great blast of out-of-key trumpets, they began kicking one another's shins. Their only defense was trousers and such straw as they'd been able to tie to their own legs. The contest continued until the defeated finally declared, "That's enough for today." The crowd went wild, a fair amount of money changed hands among the various bettors, and the next pair was called forward.

"I can't believe that grown men have been doing this here for over four hundred years," Jane sounded disgusted.

"Since five years after the founding of Jamestown, Virginia. It's—"

"I know that tone. Don't even think about it, Mason." The crowd was packed so tightly that he stood directly behind Jane with his arms wrapped around her waist and watching over her shoulder. She'd slid her arms over his, partly because there was nowhere else to put them in the press of the crowd, and partly, he guessed, because she wanted him to know what heaven felt like. His arms full of Jane Tully. Their bodies pressed together so tightly that he could feel her speak and laugh before he could hear her.

"Yes, ma'am." He actually had been considering entering the contest, which the mind-reading Jane would of course know. But having to let go of her in order to indulge himself wasn't really an option.

After the best man had won—best man in this case perhaps closely tied to cognitive dysfunction or too much alcohol—they headed for the food stalls. They ranged down a whole side of the meadow in crowds so thick it was hard to see what was being served.

"Watch the locals," Jane prompted.

"Leave it to a process specialist," but Aaron did. The active participants stood out by being dressed in costumes for the day. Even the shin-kickers had dressed as rustic peasants of old. Tourists flocked to fish and chips, pork pies, beef pasties, and Scotch eggs. But the knights errant, standing out with the elegant plumage on their steel helms, were invariably going to a small booth to the far right along with the rest of their attendant courts and servants.

They were already in line before he noticed what they were serving.

"Uh, you sure about this, Jane?"

"What?"

"Pulled lamb sliders."

"So?"

"They're made with…" Aaron couldn't think of any way to be subtle about it, "…lamb."

"And?"

"As in this year's spring lambs that they didn't need for next year's breeding season."

"Oh." And most of the color drained out of her face.

"We can go somewhere else."

"No," she shook her head and resolutely took a step forward when the line moved. "We bought lamb chops at the butcher's just two days ago. Even if I didn't think of it, I live here now. I'm going to eat like the locals."

Aaron decided to keep to himself what he saw on the rest of the sign; instead he needed to distract Jane from reading it for herself. He started by kicking her lightly on the shins.

The others in line laughed and cheered as they started their own version of the shin-kicking contest right there—thankfully done with the sides of the sneakers and not very hard. Though Jane was escalating and he was glad when they reached the stall.

"SLIDERS WITH *WHAT?*" Jane definitely needed her hearing checked.

"South Carolina barbeque sauce," the stall's proprietor answered cheerfully but she must be hearing it wrong. He was like the comedy-relief sidekick in a movie: mid-twenties, blond, just a little disheveled, with an outrageously English accent.

Aaron was grinning like a lunatic and pointing upward. There, clear as day on the sign, it said that there was nothing wrong with her hearing: Lamb Sliders—"with *Genuine* South Carolina BBQ sauce!"

She could smell it now that they were close. The breeze had

been from behind them and kept her from smelling the bite of vinegar, the tang of mustard, and the rich depth of cooking meat. Then she understood why Aaron had worked to distract her in the line.

"You!" She turned on him.

"Yes?" Aaron raised his eyebrows like Mr. Innocent, which didn't fool her for a second.

She kicked him in the shins—sharply this time. As he yelped, she turned back to the merchant. "Two servings, please. And a couple of sodas."

"Is there a problem?" The man looked worried.

"Not for you. Only for him," she aimed a finger at Aaron, who was still rubbing his shin. "I'm from Charleston, South Carolina, and he did his best to hide what you served from me." Aaron was finally upright again, so she kicked his other shin and received both a very satisfying second yelp and a huge smile from the merchant.

"South Carolina? Charleston? Oh, that be music to me ears, luv. Here! Here! Ye've got to try this. Tell me if I done it right. I spent a month tromping all over the Carolinas eating not a thing but barbeque. In August! Had me no idea how crazy an idea *that* was. I had the vinegar-and-pepper up north."

"Too thin," she couldn't help getting swept up by his enthusiasm as his assistant helped the next in line.

"Absolutely. And that ketchup they be using out west and into Kentucky I never understood."

"Me either."

Aaron had recovered, but when she cocked back her foot, he dodged back, nearly creaming a court jester in a three-pronged hat complete with little bells at the tips. She enjoyed the bright tinkle of the little bells as the two of them tried not to plummet to the ground.

"I finally settled on the lovely Carolina Gold sauce, which is from right in your Charleston. I done changed half the Dijon mustard to Colman's to bring out English flavor and more heat to the vinegar. And I use an artisan-distilled local malt vinegar for a wee bit more depth. You must tell me if I've strayed too far—I keep worrying about that, I do. I bake me own rolls 'cause I wanted something heartier than white and not as dense as brown. I've never served a native Carolinian before. I find my nerves are suddenly gone dodgy." He gasped in a breath, perhaps his first in the entire speech.

She was about to protest that she was no expert when Aaron took one of the sliders and bit into it.

"Oh, my god," he mumbled around a mouthful. "That's so good! I'm not a native like she is, but wow!"

Now Jane understood what her role was here. Compliment the man on his research and testing. He'd clearly put his heart into the meal. Once she bit into one, it wasn't hard. It wasn't like any BBQ she'd had in Charleston—it was better. "Wow!" She felt as if she was just mimicking Aaron, but it was sufficient. The man lit up as if they'd just introduced him to the girl of his dreams.

She glanced at Aaron, but he was happily chowing down on another monstrous bite and thankfully couldn't mind-read that latest thought.

Was *she* the girl of *his* dreams?

Hard to imagine that being true of her for anybody. Yet "dating" and the phrase "practically living together" were both being bandied about today. She knew she was just unnerving herself, but couldn't figure out how to stop it.

Jane took another bite of the delicious slider and knew that was the answer, the same she'd given to Aaron: *Shut up and eat your goddamn slider.*

~

AARON TRULY REGRETTED TURNING down the footraces, especially the five-miler. That one was just long enough that a soldier's ground-eating pace had a chance of pounding the sprinters into submission. He didn't need Jane's reminder about his knee to know that it wasn't an option.

And after someone tried to recruit Jane into the "Married Women's Footrace"—and refused to accept Jane's denials because of the way she and Aaron had been "cozying up together"—they decided it was time to go. It was done with a mutual glance of pure horror and the speed of foot worthy of any race.

Chipping Campden itself, a half mile down the hill, was a center of peace and serenity. The High Street was populated only by idlers like themselves, more interested in strolling than rushing into shops. The former wool-trading town was sleepy in the warm afternoon, especially in comparison to the lively riot continuing up on the hill.

"It's old," Jane offered the first comment since their breathless escape from Dover's Hill.

"Some of these buildings go back to the Dark Ages, though the settlement dates back to when years only had three digits in them."

"Over a thousand years," her voice dropped to a whisper. "Can you imagine a thousand years?"

"A thousand years ago, both of our ancestors could have lived right here. Columbus wouldn't be finding the new world for another five centuries. First cousins fifty generations ago. What do you think, cuz?"

"I think that's a weird thought that you should never mention again."

It really was. This day kept being a day of connections. It was supposed to be a day of fun out and about with the most amazing woman he'd ever met. Yet every turn seemed to lead to a more serious place. Or perhaps a deeper place.

To distract himself, to distract both of them, he made a point of noting everything he could about Chipping Campden. He took a photo of all four of their feet standing on the yard-across, stone medallion that marked the start of the Cotswold Way at the center of town. There was the old Market Hall, also dating back to the early 1600s, an open-arched area with a slate roof so that traders could meet out of the rain.

They ambled down the street. "Look at the door knockers," Jane pointed to one.

A bronze fox was peering at them from the center of a green door. The next had an iron cluster of lavender. The one three doors down, a rather large bumblebee.

"I'll bet they don't get many people knocking."

"The cottage's nameplate does say Bee Cottage." But Aaron certainly wasn't going to try the knocker.

By the time they'd wandered up and back, they'd identified over twenty animals and a dozen different plants as well as some abstracts that might have been someone's face or the wrong end of a dog.

"It's a pretty town…" Aaron wasn't sure what else to say for it.

"For a city girl to say this sounds rather silly, but it's too big."

"You're right. There must be at least two thousand people living here. How big is Charleston?"

"Don't remind me. A hundred and thirty thousand, I think. How big was Jay?"

"About five hundred. Same as Fosse."

"And we're right back to where we started the day. Small towns. Maybe I could get used to living in one."

"You'd better get used to it—you're buying a cottage in a small town." They walked back through town and got in the car. Aaron didn't have to ask if she was done-in for the day, he knew they both were. Never in his life had he been so aware of someone else's mood. It had been a good day, but a quiet dinner at the pub in their own familiar Fosse sounded wonderful.

~

"WHAT'S ALL THAT?" Jane should have offered to do the driving on the way back, but was just as glad she didn't have to. She'd never been one to let a man "take care of things," especially not driving. It had always been one of those areas she'd carved out from the male egos in her past. With Aaron, there was no contest so it didn't seem to matter.

"What's what? Oh. Hey! That looks fun," and he turned in before she could protest that she'd had enough fun for one day.

"But what is it?" They were almost into Moreton and the field there was filled with at least a hundred cars and a throng of people.

"It's a car boot sale."

"My car doesn't need boots."

Aaron laughed. "No, but it has a boot. That's what the Brits call a car's trunk. A 'car boot sale' is a flea market."

"Why do I want to look at someone else's crap?"

"Because," he parked the car.

Assuming she had no choice, she clambered out of the car.

"This is a flea market Cotswold-style."

And it was. There were all the normal thing: stacks of DVDs, boxes of books, bags of old silverware that no one in their right mind would want. Kids' clothes and toys lined up next to waist high vases painted in some vaguely Chinese styles. A whole series of paint-by-numbers paintings that clearly showed the evolution of a young artist from their terrible phase right through to solidly mediocre.

But there was also an entire table of cut crystal glassware including plates, serving dishes, goblets, even vases. The next had a dining room set that almost tempted her. If that table had been just a foot or two bigger, she might have gone for it.

"Hey, check this out." Aaron had moved on to the next table while she'd been considering the dining set.

Jane turned to see him holding Snoop Doggy Dogg cradled in his arms. Except he wasn't alive. She had to blink a few times before she could make sense of it. It was a near life-size, very rotund Cavalier King Charles Spaniel made of white porcelain. The statuette's finish coat was shiny and almost Snoop's exact coloring.

"We have to get this for Hal!"

"He'll love it." It made her laugh just looking at it. Aaron dickered them down from forty pounds to twenty and they each kicked in a ten.

"From both of us," he agreed.

She laughed again for the sheer joy of how perfect it was.

They were almost to the last table before she found something that she just had to have. A woman her own age, with close-cropped hair, dirty coveralls, and an I-chew-nails-for-breakfast attitude (though very pleasantly English about it), sat in front of a table of bronze door knockers.

"All historically accurate," the woman sat in a small lawn chair with her boots propped up on the end of her table. "I've taken the castings myself from all over the Cotswolds. Pour and polish them myself. Even cast the mounting screws," she waved a small baggie at them. "Strong enough steel for oak, but short enough they won't come out the back of your door."

Jane knew exactly which one she wanted the moment she spotted it.

It was heavy bronze. A small clump of lavender at the center. And craning its head around the side, a pheasant looked out to see what was going on. The whole knocker, swung up by grasping the pheasant's curved neck, raised on hinges hidden behind the lavender blossoms.

She stroked her fingers over it and pictured it hanging on the ancient door of Springs Cottage. It would be perfect.

Aaron was handing a small stack of bills to the woman.

"No, wait. This is mine. I'm buying it."

The woman, being a smart vendor, took the money and tucked it down the front of her shirt and into her bra with a grin. Then she placed the knocker in his outstretched palms before Jane could stop her.

"But…"

"This," Aaron placed it into her hands.

Heavier than it looked. It felt so real, so solid, like it was a part of the Earth itself.

"This is a gift from me to you for your cottage."

"But…"

"It is a way I can show how much these last weeks have meant to me."

Jane tried not to hear, *and for you to remember me by when I'm gone,* but she did.

He hadn't said it.

Probably hadn't meant it.

But she knew herself, and Jane knew her own track record with men only too well. She heard it loud and clear and hated herself for adding that on top of such an incredible day.

AARON HAD DEBATED on different approaches, and finally decided that launching a direct strike was the best tactic.

He led Jane into The Queen's Guard, hooked one hand around Bridget's shoulders as she was heading for the kitchen, and steered her up to the bar where Hal was chatting with Raymond the postmaster.

"We got something for the two of you," Aaron plonked the statuette of Snoop on the center of the bar just as Jane arrived at his other side.

"Lord above! It's me Snoop made of stone!" Hal plinked a finger against it.

"Why, it's perfect!" Bridget sounded equally delighted as she stroked it on the head. She turned and fetched the live Snoop from his bed by the fire and set him right on the bar facing…

himself. There was a light applause and several hearty laughs from those nearest the bar.

Jane took Aaron's hand and squeezed it hard in the way she did when she was particularly delighted by something. He squeezed back.

"We found him at a car boot sale outside of Moreton," Jane explained. "We adopted him immediately."

Snoop leaned forward to sniff his own statue. Raymond snapped a couple of pictures with his phone. Others were gathering about to see what all of the fuss was. Trent had been sitting with Manfred and helped the old man to his feet to come see. Gwyneth the butcher and her girlfriend were there. Phoebe, Reginald the earl's sheep man, even Harriet (Jane's estate agent) and her husband.

Aaron shared a smile with Jane. They'd nailed it. He gave her a one-armed hug and kissed her on the temple.

"Och! Ye gotta do better'n that, laddie," some Scotsman tourist called out from the crowd, so he did. He swept her into his arms and kissed her hard. Jane placed a hand on top of her head as if her hat was going to blow away, except she wasn't wearing one. Maybe it was to keep the top of her head from blowing away for the sheer joy they were both feeling.

There was a solid round of applause from the crowd and a blush as bright as her smile from Jane.

"You two're so sweet," Bridget sighed. "From the two of you to the two of us. Now there's something to keep me heart warm in the night."

"That's *my* job," Hal kissed Bridget to more catcalls. "But you're right."

"Yours and Snoop's," Bridget agreed, patting the old dog still sitting atop the bar facing himself.

Hal came around to kiss Jane on the cheek at the same time Bridget did the same to him.

"To the charming couple," Hal raised a glass.

"Hear, hear," roared back from the bar.

"To the—" Aaron got that far before total brain-lock kicked in.

Jane's eyes had shot wide as well.

"To the—" he couldn't get any further.

Someone pushed forward to take a photo of live and porcelain Snoop.

Aaron took a step back.

Another person shook his free hand before moving in to inspect the similarities and pet both dogs.

Aaron eased back another step and his hand around Jane's waist pulled her unresisting form with him.

Then another and one more.

They were now near the back of the crowd.

He looked at Jane.

Jane looked at him.

Without a word, they turned and bolted.

"WHAT JUST HAPPENED?" Jane couldn't catch her breath. Fosse wasn't that big. They had gone no more than a block, but she felt as if she'd just run a marathon.

"I…don't know." Aaron sounded as confused as she felt.

"We…toast…charming couple…" she was stuttering worse than a magpie.

"But it was only our first date!" Aaron protested.

Caught between terror and overwhelm, the only thing that slipped out was a half-gasped laugh.

In seconds they were holding on to each other and laughing until her gut ached.

"Oh my. Oh my." It was all she could say as she kept wiping at her eyes. "Oh my."

"Let's not do that again," Aaron managed as he gulped his way back to normal breathing.

She couldn't agree more.

"I hate to sound mundane, but what are we going to do for dinner?"

"I'm not going back in there!" Even a team of wild pheasants couldn't get her back in there tonight.

"Not a chance," Aaron looked around and pointed. "Takeaway Chinese. They're still open."

"Fine."

They stepped in and, for the moment, were the only ones at the counter.

"Your usual?" Kim greeted them like locals.

"Yes, please." Because Jane certainly couldn't make any more choices at the moment.

Kim took their money and then turned her phone around for them to see. "You two are so cute together."

Jane looked down at Kim's phone and could feel her head spinning again.

There, on the pub's social media page, was a shot of Hal, Bridget, Aaron, and her. They were all lined up behind Snoop and his statue with their arms around each other.

Jane almost didn't recognize herself. She and Aaron looked so—

"Happy," Aaron breathed.

It was nice to know that the emotion was as foreign to him as it was to her.

She wasn't some sad sack, yet that picture was so foreign.

When Kim handed over their meal, they walked through the late evening back to the cottage. Only after the door was locked and they were sitting across the apple crate that was their table could either of them speak.

"Small towns," Aaron managed.

"Uh-huh." It was the best she could do.

CHAPTER 12

Over the long week, the strangeness had worn off around town, at least a little. Aaron still wasn't sure if they were better off going into town together, where they'd be perceived as "that couple" or separately, which opened each of them up to questions.

Now it was Friday and Aaron had felt disconnected and restless all day. Jane was off to London to consult with an IRS specialist for ex-pats about some tax issue with her closed business. When he'd offered to go with her, she'd brushed it off. "I'm assured that it is simply reporting and paperwork. Nothing I can't handle. Work with Trent. Have a good time." Just as well. He didn't know squat about taxes and business finance.

Have a good time.

What did that look like without Jane around? A stone wall and a pint at the pub after work.

Life after meeting Jane? A whole different world.

Have a good time? When his head was aching and his nerves were all out of place and Jane was a hundred kilometers away and...

Enjoy himself. Yeah, right. Today Aaron's "fun" was tearing out his stone arch for the third time. Trent's method of training was infuriating, however effective. He'd wait until Aaron had spent hours, even days on raising it. But then something wouldn't be right. Trent would poke and prod it as if he was testing a side of beef. Then he'd wiggle a stone free and the whole arch would tremble.

"Uneven pressure from above. Every stone must be well pinned from both above and below. Once you're up in the curve of the arch, the sides must be controlled as well."

The next time Trent would casually lean on the outside of the arch well before it was finished, and it would tumble down into the yard.

"Far more than in a wall, every layer of an arch must be fully supported," then he'd walk away, turning back to building the low wall—leaving it for Aaron to solve, which first required removing the rock before he could try reassembling it.

That was no small task. The arch that Trent had sketched wasn't some single arc of well-balanced stones. The square base to one side started at over two feet square—a square pillar rising on its own. The other rose integrally from the wall itself—two different techniques to learn. The arch stones radiated upward like rays of the sun, well-chinked with smaller stones, then topped with a thick, stabilizing layer that mated with the large supports to either side.

The arch, just from the top of the walls up, required almost three tons of rock. Merely taking it down was a full day's task. Putting it back up over a wooden form, significantly longer.

Then he'd remove the form…and Trent would knock it down.

But with each failure, Aaron understood a little better how an arch worked at the most basic structural level. Though he was also getting damned sick of the whole build-tear down-rebuild cycle. She didn't need a goddamn arch anyway. Two big end-posts and a nice gate between should be enough for any woman. Why so damned fancy?

Simple. Straightforward. That was his way.

His way with women too. Say it straight: *Deploying tomorrow. Probably gone at least six months so don't bother waiting. Really enjoyed you.* No matter how he said it, it always pissed them off.

Why did women have to attach words to everything? He knew Jane wanted words—words that he didn't have. What did she really want from him? Easy! A new bathroom and a renovated kitchen.

What did *he* want? Why the fuck did it matter, anyway? He was just some goddamn cripple with delusions that great sex would be enough. Some stupid ass, broken soldier—cast aside like a defective unit—and left to build stone walls for an ancient sadist of an Englishman.

Aaron could recognize the Black Demon. Knew it was messing with him even if he couldn't shrug it off. At least it didn't consume him alive anymore when it came to visit.

And they didn't teach Delta to quit, so he went back to work on disassembling his arch.

Jane's text from London, "All done. All okay. Going to run some errands and be home late," was disturbing on two levels.

The word "home" jumped out of the message at him. His existence had been very itinerant since…leaving Vermont a decade ago. Even more now than when he was in the Army: no anchors, no real commitments—the B&B fit his lifestyle well. All of his choices were merely temporary, he was safely in neutral as long as he was living there. Now a woman said the word "home" and it drew him in ways he wasn't entirely comfortable with.

The other problem was that he was now on his own for dinner. After three months content to be eating alone, Jane had ruined him in only three weeks. It was hard to imagine a meal without her easy smile from across the table whether at the pub, out at their picnic rock, or sitting on the living room floor.

His phone rang as he finished tearing down the goddamned arch. This time because: "you've lost the curve, it should mirror that fold in the hill across the way." At least they were down to aesthetics rather than structure. Regrettably, Trent was right. The mismatched curve made it look as if his arch was about to slide over sideways even if it wasn't. He hadn't been careful enough about maintaining even tension as he followed the form.

"Yeah?" Aaron dumped half a bottle of water on his head and then hoped he didn't short out his phone while it was pressed against his ear.

"Sergeant Lame-brain!" Aaron knew the voice of his former commanding officer immediately. His nickname in the unit had been "Rock Man" or "Rocky"…until he got shot up.

"Captain Jack-off!"

"How the hell are you, soldier?"

Soldier stopped him cold. "Fine."

Captain Yakov Feynman cleared his throat. Neither of them spoke for a moment.

"How you doing, sir?" Aaron tried to restart the greeting he'd just killed with the effectiveness of a cruise missile.

"If you aren't a soldier, I'm sure not a sir. I'm Jack. You don't get it both ways, civvy-boy," Jack, too, did his best to lighten the mood, which Aaron appreciated. The captain had always been a first-class guy, even if he was an officer.

"We civilians can get away with all kinds of shit…sir."

"Yeah, I've heard about that. Where are you?"

"Fosse-on-the-Wold. Little town in—"

"So am I. I meant, where are you here? We gotta have a beer."

Aaron looked at the mess of his disassembled arch. A beer sounded really good at the moment. "The Queen's Guard pub on the square in ten."

"I'll be there in fifteen."

"That'll give me time to shower."

"Good! You always did stink," then Jack hung up giving him the last word, at least in Round One.

~

"WHAT THE HELL are you doing here, Jack?"

"Drinking beer with you."

"Real illuminating." Aaron focused on his beer.

The captain looked too damn good, which said he was fresh off a deployment. Aaron tried hard to not be desperately jealous and completely failed.

Yakov Feynman wore civvies, but the t-shirt was desert tan, as were his slacks. He looked ready to go into the field at a moment's notice. Every move he made had that extra sharpness, the precision of hot action recently piled atop the Delta standard of constant training. Aaron was staring at his beer, but he could feel Jack constantly assessing the room and everything else around him. When had Aaron lost that extra bit of edge? It had slipped away without him noticing.

"It's good to see you walking. Must have been hard."

Aaron shrugged. Hard didn't begin to cover it. Thanks to Jane and her insistence on PT, he was walking better now than he had in months, maybe ever since the injury itself.

But seeing Jack fresh off a deployment was reminding him of everything he'd lost. He didn't know what to do with the anger building inside him. Maybe because this *whole day* had sucked big time. At the moment, keeping it focused on his physical therapists seemed like a useful target. Worse, he knew enough to know the limits of what it could achieve. No matter how good his knee became, he'd never be field qualified again.

"Did you hear about Dodger?"

"Haven't heard about anyone in a while."

Jack scowled at him as Bridget delivered two massive baskets of beer-battered fish and chips.

"You always were a prickly bastard to have a conversation with."

Bridget's snort of laughter didn't help Aaron's mood.

"You're not helping."

"'E's right, you know. Before Jane, you had more in common with a hedgehog than a human."

"Just the way I liked it," he grumbled.

"Jane?" The captain suddenly perked up as he always did about women.

Aaron didn't need to hear this. He lumbered to his feet and went to the bar for a fresh round of beers. He asked Hal if there was any hot news coming in over the lambcam—there wasn't, the lambing season was mostly over—as if that somehow compared to a two-month deployment quietly cleaning the worst elements out of Libya. He also watched the mirror. Saw the captain and Bridget laughing together. Maybe he should have stayed to defend Jane's honor, but that would have brought up even more issues.

By the time he had the beers in hand, Bridget had moved on.

"Jane? You're dating a woman named Jane? I don't think I've ever met a Jane. Is she plain?"

"Drink your goddamn beer."

"Yes, sir," the captain saluted.

Being civilian, Aaron resisted the urge to return it. He'd mustered out as a master sergeant, definitely not a sir anyway.

"So, we're not discussing women. Fine. Let's talk about your leg."

"Let's not."

"Docs said I shouldn't be able to see the limp so much by now." All the banter was suddenly gone from Jack's voice.

Aaron looked up slowly from his meal. "Try that one again."

"Finally got your attention, didn't I?"

"You're here to check up on me."

"You were one of the best soldiers in my entire platoon and you know it. First, I look out for my men anyway, but you were something special, Mason."

"Not that it matters now."

"I'm a captain, so I'm smarter than you. That means shut up and pay attention."

There was enough of the soldier still in him that he did. There was enough civilian in him now that he wished there wasn't still so much soldier. Instead he focused on eating his fish.

"Dodger didn't dodge so good. Stepped off the side of the road for a piss outside of Kunduz and walked right onto an IED. Docs had to take his leg off above the knee because there was nothing left below that."

Aaron winced. At least he'd kept his leg. Dodger had been good, even by Delta standards. He'd gotten his nickname because he seemed to dodge through bullets even in a full-on firefight. Or maybe, it was speculated, the bullets dodged to avoid him—he was a kick-ass soldier when the shit hit the fan. Everyone around him would have rounds hammering into their armor and Dodger came through without even a nick in his outer clothing. But he should have known better than to step off the road without a K-9 sniffer dog checking it out first. Somebody should have taught him that—and both Aaron and the captain knew it.

"I talked to the docs at Walter Reed. For above-knee amputation, they can now fit him with a prosthetic that might put him back in the action within a year."

"Is that even possible?"

Jack shrugged. "A couple of Green Berets are back in and a gung-ho in the 82nd Airborne made it through the Jumpmaster School and is back in the Dustbowl as a paratrooper. Dodger would be the first to make it into Delta. Docs say that its possible and he always was a driven sumbitch. I did some checking and—"

"So to get back in all I have to do is chop off my fucking leg?" Aaron wanted back in so badly that it almost sounded like a fair trade.

The captain looked at him like he was a total idiot.

"Shit!" So Dodger was luckier than he was because he'd lost his *whole* leg at once.

"We don't hack off good meat when it's still bolted on and operational, no matter what sort of an idiot it's attached to."

Of course not.

But for one, brief, solitary second, Aaron had tasted it. The salt of hard-won sweat, the bitter after-bite of a battle's adrenaline high, the dust of Kandahar, Helmand, the Mog, and all of the other hellholes he'd fought in. He could feel the way his muscles would scream in agony at the end of a forty-kilometer hike in full gear over the Hindu Kush. The sound of an A-10's 30 mm cannon full-throated roar as it flew close cover above them.

And the heavy beat of a rescue helo coming in fast to grab his broken body and haul it away on a stretcher, to finally be replaced by the slow tick of the IV feed and the lazy beep of the heart monitor.

He tried to shake it off—cricked his neck, shook out his clenched fists. Even if they would chop it off, that would mean going back into the sterile, white-sheeted hell of a hospital. A year in rehab? A freaking year. He'd rather take on ISIS in his underwear with a water pistol.

Slowly the other sounds trickled back in. Trent, Hal, and Conrad laughing at the bar. Bridget flirting with a customer, just like any good waitress. The happy hum of a good pub on a busy Friday night.

The captain simply sat and watched him.

"Then what the hell are you doing here?"

"Offering you a way back in."

"I'm not cutting off my fucking leg."

"Not in ops. Training."

Training? Delta operators were trained by more senior Deltas. That's how The Unit was built. Guys who survived to drag their asses out of the field, rotated back to Fort Bragg between deployments to pass on what they'd learned and get more training themselves. What had he learned? Don't get your ass shot up in the Yemeni desert—or at least not just part of your leg.

Some big help he'd be.

He'd also be looked down on by the newbies as not good enough, and by the qualified operators as a symbol of failure. But he'd be back in. How sweet was that?

"I'm guessing you'll be needing some time on this."

Aaron could feel himself nodding. "When do you need an answer?"

"The offer stands as long as I'm in command."

Aaron tipped his beer to the captain in thanks. It was the most generous offer he'd ever received, except perhaps the moment when Jane Tully had offered herself to him.

The conversation wandered off to old missions and new stories through the second beer and the third. The crowd swirled in and out. He left it to the captain to keep an eye on any hot birds flocking through.

Still humming away in his head was the sound of gunfire—a thousand rounds of training in an afternoon. The quiet focus of requalifying as a sniper. The snores of his own squad as they sacked out in the back of a roaring C-130 transport on their way to a HALO parachute insertion. The high of extracting hostages or knowing that another leader of al-Qaeda and his inner cell had been sliced away.

Maybe not out on the line any more, but he *had* been good. When the SAS had asked for one of their best—The Unit had sent him. He could help. He could.

He wasn't sure when Jack had wandered away. "Have to be back in Bragg by the morning." Fort Bragg. Aaron's home for a decade, even if he'd never gotten a place outside the Delta compound. Back when he had places he *had* to be. Back when he still had a place called home.

Home. That rang another bell. Someone talking about "home." He managed to muzzle the memory with another pint before it could surface.

Aaron vaguely remembered an argument with Hal over how much beer was enough.

He wasn't sure when Jane came into the pub looking for him. It was quiet by then. The glass in front of him empty. He remembered her leading him upstairs, but he didn't remember anything else.

CHAPTER 13

J ane had watched Aaron all week with a growing pinch on her heart. Something had happened that night she'd been gone. What was it? And why had she stayed in London?

Her stupid errand had been to spend a couple hours walking through Harrods. She'd happily spent the time imagining just what pots and pans to get, picking out the right headboard for a bed they'd be sharing as soon as the bedroom was redone, deciding what she did and didn't want for a desk. The cottage wasn't ready for any of it yet. The only thing she'd purchased was a set of dish towels for the kitchen, printed to look like limestone walls.

Aaron's monotone response? "Nice."

She'd built a world of foolish dreams after three weeks together. One getting acquainted and two of them as lucky lovers. Week Four was turning into a classic Jane Tully-style train wreck, but usually she knew why. And she didn't want to just let it go this time. What they'd had was real. She knew it! Could feel it in her bones!

Her dream world had been one that included Aaron...until he'd stopped talking. The intimacy of their first three weeks together faded as well. Her attempts to find out more met with limited success.

"Is it something I did?" A grunt of "No, you're perfect. It's just me." Then silence.

"Is there another woman?" His look that said she was crazy to think such a thing. As if.

A week of it was enough to drive her crazy. Finally desperate and before she tipped over into stark raving lunacy, she walked over to Fosse Manor. The rain started when she was halfway there and, by the time she arrived, she was more drowned rat than the potential guest of an earl, despite having worn a light jacket.

At the door she lost her nerve. Remembering the earl's kindness after the wedding, in the lambing shed, and over their several shared pub meals, wasn't enough to see her past the presumption of her visit. She turned aside toward the front garden. She'd found some peace there once, though she couldn't quite remember how. There was no peace at the cottage, nor at the pub—both were too thick with memories of when Aaron had still been speaking to her.

She was halfway through the garden when it came back to her. She'd found peace sitting with Aaron on the stone wall by the stables. She remembered the heat of his kiss in the moonlight, the taste of chocolate cake on his lips.

The bench leapt out at her. Actually, it probably hadn't moved since the time of Queen Victoria, but one moment she was stumbling past the yew hedge and the next she was collapsing on the bench after barking her shin so hard against it that she cried out. Clasped hands over the scrape were soon warm with the blood seeping through her soaking-wet slacks. All she could do was hold on to her shin and let her tears mix with the rain, which mixed with the blood.

She cried out again when a hand touched her shoulder. The

earl stood over her in a long black raincoat far more sensible than her windbreaker. His massive umbrella sheltered them both from the chilly downpour that had soaked her to the bones.

"I'm sorry to barge in on you unannounced," was the first thing she thought to say through choked sobs and sniffles.

"Nonsense, my dear. You are always welcome," the earl assured her. He offered his arm as if he was about to escort her onto the wedding dance floor rather than finding a bedraggled mess in his garden. He escorted her through French doors into his office and ordered tea, towels, a robe, and a bandage.

He waved her to an adjoining bath to change. The maid who delivered the tea whisked away her soaking clothes. The earl sat her down in front of the warm fire that crackled happily and filled the room with warm light on a gloomy day. To her chagrin, she could see out the window that the rain had moved on and the afternoon was already brightening. He bandaged her shin himself, which had stopped bleeding, mostly.

"Well, my dear, it seems that you and Aaron will now have matching limps for a short while."

It was too much and she was crying again.

The earl provided a handkerchief and some friendly pats on the shoulder. He also waited patiently until she could force herself to regain control. She didn't cry often, except sometimes alone in the shower where no one could see or hear her. But a memory stabbed of weeping on Aaron's shoulder along the shadowed footpath to the manor. Weeping because it had felt safe enough in his arms to let it all out. Which only made now even worse when she didn't feel safe at all. It was the heat of her embarrassment that finally stopped the flow.

"I need help and I don't have anyone else to turn to."

"Glad to assist if it's within my power."

Jane started sensibly, noting that something had changed abruptly with Aaron last Friday and she didn't know what it was about. Within moments, despite her best efforts to fight it down, she was spilling out the worst of her fears. There was something wrong with her, there just had to be. It was the only explanation. And she'd known it all along. There always had been and always would be because she was such an oddity, a weak woman who—

"I think that's enough of that," the Earl of Evenston cut her off in a severe tone.

"I'm sorry." She should never of come here. "I'm so sorry. I'll just go now. I'm—" Jane began rising to her feet to escape from her mortal embarrassment. But how was she to walk back through the rain in a borrowed robe? And where was she supposed to go? How—

"Sit *down*, Ms. Tully."

Her knees went out from under her and she had no choice. The red leather creaked as she landed on it like a sack of potatoes.

"I meant that was enough of thinking that the fault lies with you. I can't imagine that to be possible."

She buried her face in her hands. How little he knew. She was such a wreck, useless, and watching Aaron…decay through the week had only served to assure her that she was right in her self-assessment. When she finally dared to look up, he was holding out a cup of tea and wore a kindly smile. She took it and stared down at it as she balanced it on her knees.

"Drink some tea," he ordered.

The strong mint did little to ease her tight throat, but it did remind her what warmth was once like. At least before Aaron's chill had—

"As it happens, I know for a fact that it wasn't you."

Jane could only blink at him in surprise.

"I was in the pub last Friday," the earl explained softly. "Your friend shared dinner with a man who might have been his brother. Oh, he wasn't. The man was smaller and blond, but he was clearly military. I perhaps should have said brother-in-arms."

"But why… What happened?"

"For the answer to that, you'll have to ask Aaron. All I know is that he was a different man by the end of that meal. The tables around him didn't refill, despite the pub being busy. I believe that, in his parlance I might say, his changing mood established a no-fly zone that encircled his position for a fair ways around. Only he and the military man he sat with know what transpired."

"But he's stopped speaking to me."

The earl offered her a plate of chocolate shortbread cookies (she hadn't been here long enough to think of them as biscuits), but she could only shake her head. He took one himself, sat back, and dunked it in his tea. "Well, if—"

"Connie, your son is being impossible!" Debbie burst into the office without knocking. She wore a Dior riding outfit: leather boots, tight pants, and a flowing black silk blouse. Jane didn't think she'd ever touched a horse and certainly wasn't likely to go riding in the rain. "Oh, well, look who's still in town."

Then she walked past Jane until she was standing between them and facing the earl. That left Jane faced with her sister's butt and Debbie knew it.

"Without my permission, your son—"

"Is not my problem anymore," the earl cut her off, showing none of that patience he'd been offering to Jane mere moments before. He set down his teacup and cookie and folded his hands. Suddenly, the sympathetic kind man transformed into a Peer of the Realm. "You are his wife now and he is now yours to manage…as you can."

Jane couldn't believe her presumption that she'd ever thought to bring her trivial personal problems before such a man as the Earl of Evenston. He was wholly unrecognizable from the man who had nursed a ewe in the lambing shed or shared a pint in the pub.

"Christ, Connie. You sound just like her," Debbie tossed her head in Jane's direction before turning to face her straight on. "What are you still doing here anyway? Isn't your precious little business back in the States missing you? All you ever seem to talk about is consulting this and systems that."

"I live here now."

Debbie, of course, had completely glossed over the failure of Jane's business. It wasn't about her, so Debbie probably hadn't even heard.

"I'm buying a cottage." Jane instantly wished she could grab the words back out of the air but it was too late.

"Well, isn't that cozy." Debbie tone was deeply insinuating as she made a show of looking down at Jane's robe and then over to the earl and back.

Jane could hear the implied *Jane, you ignorant slut!* phrase even if Debbie didn't give it voice.

"Wait," her sister's eyes narrowed. "Here in Fosse? Well, all the better that we're shaking off the dust of this dreary place. Geoffrey bought us the nicest little penthouse condo in central Milan, just five bedrooms, but the living room and view are to die for."

"Good for you." Jane really didn't want to get into any of this now. Or ever again.

"A cottage here, you say?" Debbie never forgot anything she could use as a weapon. Experience had taught her that Debbie saw everything as a threat or an opportunity to ruin Jane's life, but she couldn't think of any way to unsay the words.

"Geoffrey," the earl's tone was suddenly both imperial and dismissive, "will be easier to control in Milan. There are more... diversions." His tone managed to imply mistresses and that Debbie was little more than a bought-and-paid-for one of those. How he did that without varying his tone, Jane was unsure, but Debbie's face flushed red hot.

She sniffed, made a point of giving Jane the finger out of the earl's line of vision, and strutted back out of the room with her hips in full sway.

The office echoed with the slam of the door. They sat

unmoving until the click of Debbie's boots had disappeared across the marble hallway and everything was once again quiet.

"I believe," the Earl of Evenston picked up his teacup, dunked his biscuit, and offered her a friendly smile that would have been unimaginable seconds before. "We were discussing Aaron's newfound reticence."

Jane wanted to start crying again in thanks for the kind and understanding man. "Thank you, your lordship."

"Conrad, at least."

"Conrad," she finally assented. "You are the best of men."

"I might pursue that, despite our age difference, if you weren't so in love with Aaron Mason."

"I might not mind, if you weren't right." The words were out before she could stop them. In *love?* With Aaron? He was stubborn, close-mouthed, scaring the shit out of her and… and…

And she was *totally and completely* in love with him.

"But…" was all she managed.

"Obvious the moment you walked into the wedding on his arm, I must say. Quite the most charming couple I've seen in a long time."

"He was being my White Knight, protecting me from…" Jane didn't need to finish the sentence.

"And you were his Queen," Conrad agreed complacently as if the ground wasn't shifting under her feet.

"That's what *he* said." Jane did her best to manage a single breath but inside it felt more like another sob. "At least I was, before everything changed."

"WHAT THE HELL happened to you, boy?"

Aaron glared at Trent but didn't speak.

"Look at it. Really look."

Aaron turned his glare on the arch. "It's just a goddamn stone arch. Why does it have to be so fucking perfect?"

"Perfect?" Trent practically shouted at him. "My granddaughter could make a better one with her building blocks."

Aaron had spent five days working on it while Trent was off visiting his kid and grandkid. He'd forced the thing into form and position. He'd…

"Do I have to show you?"

If Trent showed him what was wrong with the arch, Aaron wouldn't be accountable for his own actions.

It was just fine! If he ignored the curvature. And the leaning toward the footpath. So tipsy that the rain might take it down. And the shoddy base layer that wasn't going to stand any better than a half-crippled man in a firefight.

Dodger had lost his leg, so he'd get to stand tall again.

Whereas Aaron was merely a sad gimp who—

He grabbed the keystone and yanked.

It was stuck hard.

He yanked it again. His hands, slick with mud, slid off the stone. He grabbed it harder.

"No! Don't—" Trent shouted, but Aaron got it free. The suddenly free keystone slammed into his chest, knocking him away and flat onto his back in the trampled grass and soggy mud. It was probably the only thing that saved him.

The whole upper curve of the arch gave way in a single, flowing wave of limestone. He couldn't crawl away fast enough and it piled down on him. Rocks battered into him. Gut. Hip. Leg.

When a particularly large stone caught his bad knee, all he could do was scream. Whether it was pain or rage he didn't know.

Jane yelped when her cell phone rang.

The maid holding her clothes still warm from the dryer looked at her strangely.

Conrad nodded that it was okay and she answered the unknown number.

"Where are you?"

"Trent?"

"I'm at the cottage. You'd best get here fast."

CHAPTER 14

The first thing Aaron noticed was the smell. Hard, biting, antiseptic.

Crisp sheets.

A feeling he was undressed…except for the small pressure of an all-too-familiar knot at the nape of his neck. Hospital gown. He was in a goddamn hospital. Again!

That's when it registered that everything hurt. His chest, his hip, his—

Falling stone!

Aaron jolted up. "My leg! Do I still have my leg?" Two lumps under the sheet, thank god, not one. One was fatter than the other but at least there were two of them. He tried flexing his feet. One moved the sheet, the other met resistance and he could barely wiggle his toes. The familiar, choking embrace of a leg cast. Everything from his knee down began to itch all at once but that feeling too was an old acquaintance, perhaps even a friend. At least his leg was still there.

A face moved into his line of vision and took his hand for half an instant, then let go.

Jane. She always looked so put together in her slacks so neat they looked freshly pressed and a blouse that flowed softly over her.

Then he remembered the arch. Clawing at it like a madman. So angry that it boiled out of him until…until it had collapsed on him. He was damned lucky to be alive.

He flopped back on the pillow and wished he hadn't. He closed his eyes as the world swirled viciously and the major bump on the back of his head throbbed from the impact with the pillow.

"How bad?"

"They called it a non-displaced fracture. You cracked your shin bone badly, but nothing shifted."

"No worse a cripple than I was before?"

"No worse," her voice was barely a whisper.

"Goddamn it," but he couldn't find the heat of fury that had burned so deep in him for so long. Was it gone too? Abandoning him as fast as Jane would if she had any sense of self-preservation. Or had the Black Demon merely been knocked out cold by the falling rock, as he had, and would attack again all too soon?

"You *want* it to be worse?" Her voice was a shocked whisper. She hadn't run yet.

"Yes. No. I don't know." And he really didn't. But he could do without that damned heart monitor beeping away the last seconds she'd ever tolerate being near him.

"Why would you *want* to be injured?" She moved a step away and he missed her. It would kill him if she actually went—he knew that, yet could do nothing to stop her as his final seconds beeped by.

Aaron still didn't know if he'd be happier without his bad leg. Hadn't been able to think of anything else since the captain's offer to return as a wounded trainer.

"Aaron!" Jane's voice was sharp, sharper than he'd ever heard it.

He opened his eyes and looked at her. "Your eyes are red."

"Duh!"

Okay, perhaps not his smartest opener. She'd been weeping and it had been his fault, which sucked.

"What happened last Friday? Who was that man and what the *bloody hell* did he say to you?" It wasn't like her to swear.

Aaron shrugged.

Jane stepped in and thumped the center of his chest with the side of her fist.

"Ow! Shit!"

Pain radiated outward from where the first stone had pummeled him. The pain slammed into the knot on the back of his head where he must have knocked himself out by tumbling backward.

"I might have cracked a rib or two while I was at it." He tested with a deep breath and decided they were only bruised, but her blow still hurt.

"I'd say I'm sorry, but I'm not. Now tell me."

It was the red eyes that finally persuaded him. He could see the pain there. In hindsight, he could see that he'd been causing it all week, which made him a total heel.

"I can't believe you're still here." But he didn't pause for a response he was afraid he wouldn't like. He told her about Jack's visit and the way Aaron envied Dodger his second chance. Everything. Including the opportunity to get back in, if only he was willing to totally swallow all of his pride and be the resident gimp-boy that no one would ever truly respect.

"Back in?" Jane had sat on the edge of the bed, her hip against his good thigh, separated only by a sheet and his stupid hospital gown. She wouldn't do that if she was planning to run, would she? He prayed not.

"With The Unit. Delta. Back as a trainer, if not in action." Darkness out the window, TV off, door to the hall closed. There was nowhere to look except at Jane.

"That's why you wanted to lose your leg? Has an amputee ever made it back into Delta?"

"No, though a few Green Berets have and a jumper in the 82nd Airborne. But the docs say it can be done. Got a recently injured buddy who lost one," Aaron slashed a hand across his mid-thigh, "and is going for it."

"And you want to do this?" Jane's question, and her face, were both painfully blank. He couldn't read a thing about her reaction. No guideposts for the damned—she was leaving him to find his own answers. And if she didn't like the answer? He couldn't think about that.

Did he want it? "I'll be damned if I know."

He could see her swallowing hard.

"Go on, ask the question," he prompted her.

She shook her head, sending a shower of hair to cover her face. He reached up to brush it aside, but she flinched away. He guessed that he deserved that no matter that it hurt worse than his head, ribs, or the leg that was now bringing its own complaints online. So, he took a stab in the dark…not that it was so mysterious now that he was flat on his back instead of trying to hide behind all the rage. He could read the question in her red eyes and the hunch of her beautiful shoulders.

"No. It's not because I want to get away from you."

No reaction.

"Seriously. I'm not that stupid. You're incredible."

Her shoulders sagged the tiniest bit in relief and he heard her take a hard breath from behind her golden shield. This time she didn't flinch when he brushed her hair back over her shoulder.

"No man in his right mind would want to get away from you."

"That makes you a first, not that I'm complaining about your bias. Then what *is* the problem, Aaron?" He could hear both the desperation and exasperation clear in her voice. Just how much had he put her through this last week? Way more than she deserved or should have to tolerate.

Shit!

He had to stare at the ceiling fluorescents for a long time

trying to puzzle out the problem. He reached out and made sure to have a firm hold on her hand so she couldn't slip away while he was working on it. The reassurance when she finally returned his grip was startling in its depth.

"The problem..." he muttered up at the fluorescents, "is..." he wasn't getting anywhere. "The problem is...I don't *want* to lose my damned leg, even if I had it to do over. And now that I'm actually doing my PT, it's fine for civilian use, or it was until I did this. I've adapted, mostly. Losing my leg isn't an answer. Going back in as the outcast and unwelcome trainer isn't any better. But if I'm not Delta, then who the hell am I? That's what I can't figure out."

"That's easy."

He could only blink in surprise at her as she smiled down at him. It was a sad smile, but it was perhaps the first one he'd seen in a week.

"You're the man that I love."

She sounded utterly confident, but she looked as shocked as he felt.

CHAPTER 15

Jane went out of her way all week to make him feel that he hadn't totally screwed up the week before. Again proving that no idiot in his right mind would run away from her.

Aaron kept trying to apologize and she kept telling him to shut up until he finally got the message and did.

While riding along with Trent on some errands—just so he had something to do—he found her a nice vase down in Bourton-on-the-Water. Actually it was a heavy ceramic water pitcher but decorated with sweet peas, which he figured made it vase-like at least. He left it in the living room, overflowing with tulips from Fosse's third-Friday-of-the-month farmer's market. He pictured her finding it when she got back from her own errands.

For reasons beyond his imagining, Jane loved him.

He could feel it in the cottage. Could see it in the air mattress they still shared though he didn't deserve it. Could touch it in the dining set she'd purchased because he could no longer sit on the floor comfortably while wearing a cast.

He crutched his way out into the garden. The sun was out and it felt good to be out in it again. He levered himself down until he was sitting on their impromptu stone table and set his crutches aside. The lambs in the meadow on the far side of the Heart of England Way footpath were growing and soon more males would be culled into lamb chops.

Aaron breathed in the air and tried to understand how he hadn't been culled out of the herd. Shot up—he'd been saved by a medic. Buried in stone—Trent had dug him out.

And Jane…

Jane had said she loved him.

What was a guy supposed to do with that?

Aaron needed a distraction, badly. It wasn't hard to spot one as he looked toward the fallen arch.

Per his instructions, Trent hadn't touched a thing. Aaron surveyed the rubble. He *had* been lucky to survive. Stone was scattered everywhere and there was a grim outline of where he'd been partially buried, thankfully clear of the very worst of it or he'd be dead by now. He shifted to sit on the grass near the most scattered stones and began tossing them back into their various piles by size. Each time he cleared what he could reach, he scooted his butt over and went back to his sorting.

After a week, the bump on his head had healed and his ribs were only frustratingly sore. Any Delta knew how to ignore that —even a former one.

And Jane had said she loved him.

She managed not to look too hurt when he didn't say it back. Which only moved him deeper into that the foreign terrain of no man's land that lay somewhere past *like,* but before that other word.

Last person he'd said that to other than his mom was Mary back in high school. She'd rolled her eyes, though he'd meant it at the time. She'd been amused and explained the difference between teenage love and true love. She'd always been the deep thinker of the two of them.

A magpie, so formal in its black-and-white feathers, landed

atop the broken wall for a moment. It inspected him, the wall, the blue sky, and him again with quick twists of its head. With a shrug that said everything was as it should be, it fluttered away. A pair of sparrows did a brief dance down along the edge of the trench, snatching up a few bugs before taking flight. For the first time in weeks he became aware of the birdsong that always seemed to fill the Cotswolds, like nature's answer to elevator music.

"What are you doing?" Jane had come down the garden path from behind him while he tossed rock.

"Cleaning up my mess. I'm sitting. No stress on the leg, nurse."

"You're such a good boy," she leaned down and kissed him on top of the head.

He reached both arms over his head for her, but she scooted away. Overbalancing, he landed on his back, with a rather painful fist-sized rock poking into his kidney. He cleared it and looked at her upside-down.

She clutched the sweet pea vase to her chest and her face was framed to either side by the wildly varied tulip colors. Jane made a show of hugging it tighter. "You're *such* a good boy." Even upside down her smile was brilliant.

"Your secret's out, you know," Aaron pushed himself upright and turned around to face her.

"What secret?"

"You're a total sucker for flowers."

"From the right man, I sure am."

He tossed a few more rocks. "The right man...how do you know?" The question was out before he could stop it.

"How do I know that I love you?"

At his nod, she sat down on the lawn still clutching her vase and flowers.

"What kind of a question is that, Aaron? You either know or you don't."

"Not real helpful."

~

THE BEAUTIFUL VASE was digging into her chest so hard that it hurt.

"How can you not know?" *How can you not know, yet still pick out such a perfect gift?*

Aaron grimaced. "This is new territory for me, okay? A soldier's life is a very unsettled one. There are a couple of female Deltas now, but I haven't ever met one. So I hung out with guys for a living and occasionally hooked up with a base clerk or a bar-babe for a while. But that's about it."

"And you want me to explain what love is?" Her and fifty centuries of poets right back to Homer.

"Too tall of an order?"

"Would you like a kick in the shins?"

"You'll just hurt your foot if you kick me in the cast."

She stuck her tongue out at him but felt better than she had in a while. She'd forgotten just how good the good days could be with Aaron, but that day just out exploring had been so exceptional that—

"How about why you think—"

At her scowl, he cleared his throat.

"—how you *know* that you're in love."

"With you," she emphasized.

"Uh-huh." Aaron picked up a nearby rock and tossed it negligently onto one of the piles. She was pretty sure it was the wrong pile, which told her just how much he cared about this conversation despite his pretended indifference. "You do know that, if you were any other woman, that would make your sanity suspect for choosing me out of the herd?"

"Trust me, I know." She'd arrived at the same time as the ambulance and couldn't believe the mounds of rock that Trent had moved aside as Conrad had raced the pink Ferrari through Fosse like a Formula One driver. It had looked like the chalk outline of a corpse, in limestone piles over a foot deep. She really needed to figure out which saint to thank that Aaron wasn't dead. His face and the rest of his body still showed the signs of various cuts and bruises, which he shrugged off as if they were somehow too normal to even be noticed.

The terror of finding out that she loved him and then nearly losing him in the same fifteen minutes still shook her to the core.

How did she know she loved Aaron? Conrad had said as much and she'd simply walked into the trap.

"Because it's true."

Aaron began tossing more rocks aside. Jane reached out and grabbed the bare toes sticking out the end of his cast to get his attention.

She looked into those deep, revealing eyes of his and could see the worry there. Jane had never doubted, except for that one week, that Aaron enjoyed being with her. But now she could see that it went much deeper. Is that what Conrad had seen so clearly? She could see it in Aaron and she didn't think it was wishful thinking. However, pushing him wasn't going to help.

"Give it time," she managed though her heart longed to hear it now. "Just give it time."

He opened his mouth to say he was sorry, but she held up a hand to stop him.

Aaron grimaced, "Right. Sorry doesn't help shit. I've got that."

Actually it helped a great deal, but sometimes Aaron used it like a cudgel on himself that was very hard to stop.

She carefully set aside her beautiful vase, making sure it was stable on the little stone table Aaron had built for them a lifetime ago, then moved forward and kissed him. For the first time since the pub dinner with his captain, he returned it like he really meant it.

"Come on," she fetched his crutches and helped him to his feet.

She led him back to the cottage where they made slow love through the long afternoon.

CHAPTER 16

The knock on the door rousted them both from the air mattress. Aaron checked his watch—eight a.m. on a Saturday. That wasn't even decent.

He lay still for a moment while Jane scrabbled around for her clothes—a sight he would never tire of. He might not know if he was in love but, getting to wake up each day next to a naked Jane, he did know that he was the luckiest damn guy ever.

"*Aaron,*" Jane's hiss was a little frantic. The front door did open into the living room, so he got her point. Besides, her blouse and shorts were on now and she was brushing out her hair as she called out for the visitor to hold on.

He yanked on his own clothes and helped her toss the sheet and blankets into some shape. The air mattress had definite limitations. Sale or no sale, the master bedroom was next on his list. He wanted Jane in a king-size bed so badly he could hardly think of anything else at the moment.

"Oh. Good morning, Harriet," Jane was at the door, completely polite and looking as put together as ever. "We weren't expecting you."

An estate agent at eight in the morning. Well, maybe the

cottage was finally Jane's and they could get down to the bigger repairs at long last.

"I have news that I thought I should bring by in person."

Aaron still felt all rumpled and only half awake. He waved as he crutched by into the kitchen to start some tea. He really needed to remember to buy some coffee.

The cry of dismay from the living room had him racing back.

Harriet was looking at the floor and Jane had gone sheet white.

"What? What is it? Did someone die?" He doubled his crutches under one arm and wrapped the other around Jane's waist.

So warm and soft as she slept against him moments ago, she was now shivering and as rigid as steel.

"Are you okay?" Stupid question. Try again. "What happened?"

Jane finally waved a hand helplessly at the estate agent.

"Two problems. The financing fell through because Ms. Tully is no longer employed."

"I have the cash," Jane whispered. "It means liquidating some investments, but I have the cash."

"And the owner," Harriet cleared her throat delicately, which was the English version of a severe epithet, "has used that opening to raise the price of sale."

"Is that legal?"

"It's…terribly crass," she chose her words carefully. "But it *is* legal."

"How much?"

She showed him the number. No wonder Jane was in shock—it was over half again the asking price.

"That's an odd amount." It wasn't half, two-thirds, or three-quarters of the original listing price. In fact, it had digits right out to pence. "How much is that in US dollars?"

Harriet pulled out a calculator, tapped in the amounts, and showed them. "That is at today's valuation." Which told him that the seller was American—it was an even dollar amount, though it was still a strange number.

"I can't afford that, Aaron. What am I going to do? It would almost wipe me out. I could buy the cottage but then I couldn't afford to live here for very long."

Aaron couldn't imagine Jane anywhere else. The cottage was so perfect for her. Their talk of the renovation had made the place so real that he couldn't imagine being anywhere else either. That had been part of his problem last week. He wanted Delta. But even more than that he wanted to be here with—

"Ha!"

"What?"

He shook his head, "I'll tell you later." He finally got what Jane had been saying. What if love was when you couldn't imagine being with anyone else—ever? If that was the right question, then he already knew the answer.

Well, if the right place for him was here with Jane, he'd be damned if some greedy son-of-a-bitch landowner was going to take it away.

"If she accepts today, that locks in the price? He won't be able to increase it again."

"Yes," Harriet nodded. "This is his counter-offer. Once you accept it, the price negotiation is complete. If Jane counters at a lower price, he could choose to increase it again. Or walk away from the deal."

"Okay. Jane, sign it."

"I just said I can't. Weren't you listening?"

He cursed his crutches for the hundredth time this week as he tried to turn her to face him.

She finally looked up at him with those green eyes he could watch forever.

"*We* can afford it."

Her eyes widened briefly. They didn't change at his nod, but she mechanically took the pen and signed with a flourish.

Harriet was watching them closely, but didn't say a word before she left.

"How long do you think *that* news will take to sweep through town? By end of morning or until sometime this afternoon?" He tried to make it a joke, but Jane's wide eyes were still watching him so closely.

"Really, Aaron?"

"Really."

"What…" the single word ran Jane out of breath.

"What changed?"

She managed a tiny nod.

"I can't imagine ever meeting a better person to spend the rest of my life with."

Again the tiny nod of agreement.

The words, doofus. He took a deep breath as if he needed as much air for three little words as he did before diving out of an airplane. The image was too funny and he started to laugh.

Jane's smile slowly grew.

He was the most ridiculous person he'd ever met, but those weren't the words she needed, waited for. He wanted to pull her against his chest, crush her there so that she could never leave, but he needed to see her eyes when he was finally able to speak.

So he waited until he could get his breath under control.

Waited until the mood was again quiet and his world was filled by her half-formed smile and her brilliant, shining eyes.

"I love you, Jane Tully."

The tears running down her cheeks were the only answer she managed.

It was more than enough.

The next weeks were frantic with banks and setting up a mortgage. With Aaron's savings and his job, they were back to being able to finance the purchase. Every step forward was like slogging through mud until Jane thought she was going crazy. She would have, if she wasn't so happy.

She'd downloaded the picture of her and Aaron with everyone else at the bar that night and made it the background on her phone. Any time she felt that the world was winning, she would go into the bathroom, look at the phone and then up at herself in the mirror. The two images were coming into alignment.

Departments she'd never heard of were investigating her and Aaron's visas. Did they have the right to own land in the UK? Did they have the correct forms to work here? Did they even have the right to stay in the country?

They finished the bedroom and started on the bath. The arrival of the king-size bed and dressers had been a major celebration. Hal and Bridget had made a big fuss when she and Aaron had arrived to fetch the last of his belongings from his room at the pub. Hal had thumped her on the back hard enough to knock the wind out of her, not leaving her any way to protest as Bridget kissed both of them soundly.

She and Aaron hadn't looked at each other until everything was tucked away in drawers or hung in the small closet. The last thing she hung was the dress she'd worn to the wedding. When Aaron saw it, the heat came into his eyes and cast or no cast, he'd swept her into his arms, carried her the two steps to the bed, and they'd fallen into it together. It had been a long and glorious afternoon before they emerged again.

Inspectors came out of the woodwork ready to find something damning about the cottage. There were times they were queued up in the kitchen with cups of tea, waiting to inspect one thing or the other. The suggestion that they might add a gable and window in the third story suddenly had the District Council Trust descending on them. Renovations in the Cotswolds were tightly regulated in order to maintain an "authentic historic appearance." They were quickly followed by the National Trust. It was as if the UK didn't want them to be here, but they fought them down one by one. Some nights they'd collapse into bed too exhausted and strung out to even eat.

At the very depths of the renovation of the bathroom, they had to move back into the pub for a few days. Hal and Bridget welcomed them just as jubilantly as they had sent them off.

Aaron had shed crutches and now his cane. He was down to a walking cast, which was a great relief—though she still wouldn't be kicking his shins. Aaron cooped up, unable to work, was a definite challenge. He'd cleared the fallen arch, all while sitting on his butt. However, the thought of him working on it…

"Can't you just let Trent do it?" The thought of him back near all that stone scared the living daylights out of her, though she tried not to show it.

"It's mine to do!" Aaron's voice was practically a snarl, though she could tell it was directed at the arch and the last few feet of wall and not at her. She'd finally had to enlist Trent to shut him down, at least until he was solid on both feet.

So they'd turned to the interior renovation with a vengeance.

"Going to be time to christen this room soon," Aaron was putting the last coat of paint on where he'd removed the wall between the living room and dining room. The new beam was stained dark to match the historic woodwork. She'd selected a cross between a warm bronze and a soft gold for the walls that glowed in the sunlight.

"We need to celebrate."

"That's what I had in mind."

She kissed him on the shoulder as she walked by. "That too. I meant we should have a dinner party."

"Us?"

"Us. I want to invite Hal, Bridget, Trent, and Conrad at least."

"Well, we *are* good enough cooks now that we aren't too likely to poison them."

"I think," Jane turned slowly, unable to believe how the room looked. It didn't just look like she'd imagined, it *felt* like…home. "I think I'll bake a pie. A good authentic apple pie from that recipe your mom sent me."

Suddenly she was clamped in Aaron's arms.

"You want the way to my heart, you bake one of those apple pies."

"I thought I already was in your heart," she tried to sound offended but it didn't work very well.

"You are. But you and apple pie? That's every Vermont boy's dream come true," Aaron began nuzzling her neck.

"Hey. I thought we were going to wait for the furniture."

"Preview," he grunted as his hands clamped on to her behind and pulled her tight against him.

"You're in the middle of painting," she leaned back as he worked his mouth along her collarbone.

"Coat needs to dry," he pulled her down to straddle his lap as he sat on the top of the little stepladder just high enough to do the brush work on the ceiling.

"You're not paying attention," but then again neither was she because he was paying incredible attention to what he was doing to her body.

In the moments before he totally blanked her mind, she wondered if he'd always have this power over her.

With a soft groan she gave in to the moment and hoped that he would.

~

"AND THEN, like ruddy Arthur pulling the sword from the stone, he dropped the whole ten-foot-high arch on himself."

Aaron could have done without the tale of his idiocy told in full shining color, but Trent was unstoppable and the others around the dinner table roared with laughter. To be fair, Jane laughed politely and only paled slightly, but the others were certainly laughing. At him, not with him—which Aaron supposed he fully deserved.

Then Conrad, acting much the Earl of Evenston, told of the dusty vagabond who had walked into the poshest wedding of the season. Bridget followed with, in excruciating detail, his first meeting with Jane.

"When did this become a roast Aaron night?"

"The day you were born," Captain Yakov Feynman crowed. Jack had been passing through again, up from Dorset where he'd been for sea training with the Brit's Special Boat Service—their version of SEAL Team 6. He flirted outrageously with Jane—who haughtily informed him that they weren't on speaking terms, then hugged him for welcome to prove herself wrong. He'd also flirted with Bridget, who gave back even better than she got, despite leaning against Hal while she was doing so.

They settled into reverent silence as Jane served up fresh apple pie, vanilla ice cream, and a drizzle of caramel sauce. She'd actually made six pies in the prior week for practice until even his nostalgic appetite for apple pie was sated. Well, mostly sated.

"This is spectacular, Jane."

"He's right for once," Jack conceded. "You better marry this girl or I'm going to take her off your hands damn fast."

Aaron felt a momentary madness come over him. "Of course I'm going to marry her, so back off, Jack-off." And as they traded a laugh, his words sank in. When they finally slammed home, he spun around to face Jane.

Again, those wide green eyes inspected him carefully.

"You are?" Her voice was just a whisper in the sudden silence.

He could only nod.

"Don't you think you'd better ask first?" Jack slapped him hard on the shoulder.

He could only nod again. Then he rose to his feet, shoved his chair aside, and went down on one knee before her. The pain hit his bad knee and all he could do was curse as he switched knees.

"Do it up right, boy," Trent admonished.

Conrad was smiling and Bridget was looking like she was fighting tears as Hal wrapped an arm around her shoulders.

"Do it up right," he muttered mostly to himself in disgust.

"Yeah," Jack joined in. "Like the soldier you were and the man you are."

Aaron had to look at the captain for a moment.

Jack nodded with that short, military acknowledgement that he was sending the right man in to get the job done properly.

"Hurry it up, Aaron," Hal crowed. "Before the lass comes to her senses."

"Now I better understand Jane's instructions on when I should just *shut the hell up!*" He scowled at his friends who had the gall to just grin at him.

He turned back to Jane, reached out for one of her hands, and actually felt like a White Knight as he knelt at his Queen's feet.

"You know my skill isn't with words."

That earned him a small smile.

"But you, Jane Tully, are absolutely the woman I want to spend the rest of my life with. Will you have me, Jane? For richer, poorer, and all that?"

She managed a tiny nod that changed his world.

"Say it, girl!" Jack called out. "Say it like you mean it."

Jane glanced over Aaron's head with a look that would quell a Russian tank. Then she looked back down at him and Aaron could feel the smile all the way to his toes.

"In your vernacular, Aaron: Hell, yeah!"

Aaron laughed so hard that he had to sit down. His cast made it awkward enough that he more collapsed than sat on the floor. In a moment, his arms were full of Jane Tully. She wrapped her arms around his neck and kissed him so hard that he fell onto his back, dragging her down on top of him.

"Get a room!"

"Take a video!"

"Can I have your slice of apple pie?"

"Hell, no!" He and Jane shouted in unison and then both burst out laughing. He'd thought that making the grade at Delta Force had been a good day, but that didn't even pass muster compared to holding Jane Tully in this moment.

"You know that you two have really fixed this up a treat," Trent sat on the forest-green leather couch, a pint glass of beer clasped in both hands. Jane liked that he looked comfortable there. Tonight had made the cottage feel more like a home than she'd imagined possible. Than she'd ever had since leaving home at eighteen.

They'd lit a small fire though it was a pleasant May evening and they'd also opened the French doors to let in the last of the sunset. The bronze wall paint soaked up the warmth. She'd found some tall copper vases at a car boot sale in Cirencester that were now filled with cattails. Aaron, the ever resourceful Aaron, had shown her how to plant sunflowers so she have those in the fall. Fosse had a gardening club, that as the new owner of an English garden, she'd best join soon and learn something herself. If she had time.

"With the way the owner jacked up the price at the last minute, I'm going to have to find work as soon as the renovation is done."

"Then just keep doing it."

"Doing what?"

"Fixing up places like this," Trent waved a hand. "You got a good aesthetic eye. Aaron's about the most capable lad I've ever met, though I'd appreciate it if you didn't tell him I said so or I'll never keep him in line."

"Fixing up places like this?"

"Renovations are a big business in the Cotswolds. I can count the folks who are this good at it on my two hands and have plenty of fingers left over for holding a pint," he tipped his beer to make his point.

Jane shook her head. "I don't think I could survive the inspector storm ever again. That really set us back."

"Inspector storm?"

She described all the different bureaucrats who'd been through and what they'd insisted on, but tapered off as Trent started shaking his head.

"That doesn't sound right."

"What doesn't sound right?" Conrad turned from chatting with Aaron and Jack to face them.

She explained.

"Trent's right. That's damned peculiar."

"We just thought it was your English system to make foreigners suffer."

Trent and Conrad exchanged a look that was too easy to interpret.

"Then what was going on?"

"Sounds like someone had it in for you," Trent didn't sound happy.

"But who would…" Even as she said it she knew. "Debbie."

"Who's that?" Trent asked.

Conrad simply looked disgusted.

"Oh no! No. No. No." Jane's stomach clenched into a fist. "Aaron!"

Everyone spun to face her at her call.

"How much was that price? For the cottage?"

He named the amount.

"No. In US dollars."

Hearing the amount, it took all of her willpower to not be sick. This couldn't be happening.

In seconds he'd shoved aside the coffee table and was beside her. "What? What's wrong?"

"That…" she was so angry that she was shocked she was still capable of speech. "That is exactly the amount of profit I made when I finally had to sell Mom and Dad's house. I had already paid Debbie half of present market value to gain sole ownership. Then the market recovered while I held onto it. It's exactly how much the value went up."

"What's Debbie got to do with our cottage?"

She didn't know, but she knew she was right.

"I'M afraid I may have the answer to that." Conrad spoke tersely in his Earl of Evenston tone. Aaron had met less intimidating Delta Force commanders.

He held onto Jane's shaking hands and they all turned to listen to the earl.

"When I purchased the estate here in Fosse-on-the-Wold, a holding company came in and swept up most of the for-sale properties. The town had fallen into quite a state of disarray and prices were very favorable to an enterprising person with money."

"Geoffrey," Jane breathed it out.

"Geoffrey," Conrad confirmed. "I didn't see any particular harm in it and he hasn't done any undue price gouging. At least not prior to this. He simply had the capital to hold the properties until the market improved. Even fixed up some cosmetic problems…"

"Such as hiring me to be fixing the garden wall," Trent agreed. "You recall, Aaron, when we started it was past historical and well on its way to eyesore."

Aaron nodded, it was all he could manage.

"Yes, my youngest son has many shortcomings, but he is a smart investor who likes to make sure he receives top dollar. People can imagine renovating an interior, but a crumbling rock wall lies beyond the range of most potential buyer's imaginations."

It didn't mean that Aaron was one bit less tempted to go find the Third Worm of Evenston and wring his neck before the night was over.

"But how did Debbie—" Then Jane swore in a very unladylike way, rich enough with both British and American invective to raise a number of eyebrows including his own. "That day I was in your office, Conrad, at the manor."

"What day? What happened?"

But Jane just shook her head. Too much to explain to Aaron, especially as to why she'd been there—because of her fears about him.

"Yes," the earl agreed. "That's when you admitted to her that you were in the process of purchasing a cottage."

"What are we going to do about it?" Aaron had no problem strangling Geoffrey until he whimpered like a lost soul. He was warming up to the idea of doing the same thing to Jane's sister even if she was a woman. The only downside he could see was that it wouldn't actually achieve anything.

"Nothing," Jane whispered. Then she sat up straighter, pulled her hands from his and folded them in her lap. "We're going to do absolutely nothing," she stated in a clear voice.

Aaron could only goggle at her. "Nothing?"

"I don't want to give her the satisfaction of knowing how she's affected us in any regard. Not monetarily, not emotionally. My pain is what she thrives on and I'm done with her."

There was a respectful silence.

"So—" Aaron didn't even know where to begin. He understood her reasoning. He also knew better than to argue with his fiancée on the night of their engagement.

Old Delta training: done with a mission—for better or worse —then move on to the next one. Once the post-op briefing was done and any learned lessons had been integrated into future tactics, dwelling on the past was not constructive.

"So...what's next?"

"Well," he could see Jane fighting—and against all odds winning—the battle for calm in front of their friends.

If ever there was a woman for a warrior man, she was it. Jilted out of a third of her savings and she simply moved forward. Her inner strength never ceased to teach him the best way to be.

"Trent was discussing an intriguing proposal before... well....before." It was nice to hear the waver and know that she wasn't all steel inside.

"I thought I made it clear that I was the only one proposing tonight," he aimed a mock scowl at Trent and Jack, which didn't earn a smile, but it lightened the mood.

"A business proposal."

Aaron shook his head. "From an old dude like Trent? I can't believe you fell for that line."

It finally earned him the laugh he'd been hoping for before they all began discussing it.

~

"COME ON UP. I have a surprise for you," Aaron called from the third floor window.

As if it was a great mystery. Aaron had banished her from the top floor all week. Her office was the last unfinished room in the cottage.

"Let me clean up first," she called back.

She finished watering the soil around the new rose bushes she'd planted to frame Aaron's beautiful stone arch. In a year or two, they'd help bring the view to life. For tomorrow's backyard wedding…at least the intent was there.

A couple walked their dog along Heart of England Way and she could see them admiring the cottage and the garden. They waved and continued on their way. She waved back. She wasn't sure, but she thought they were somehow involved with the town's small library.

She turned to look at the cottage herself. It was done. With Hal and Trent's help, and the cottage as their showpiece, they already had several jobs lined up. She was the business and logistics side of their company, but Aaron had bought her a toolbelt and was teaching her how to help as well. Tearing things down and building them back up seemed to make him happiest. She liked the little touches: fine trim, brass fittings, the little things that made their cottage a home rather than just a house.

Springs Cottage Restorations was going to take a lot of hard work, but it was all theirs. And one thing she knew about being a project manager engaged to a former Delta Force soldier, they both thrived on hard work.

Aaron had also been teaching her to relax. He claimed that it was the Vermont in him coming out.

At the end of a day, they'd often sit out in the garden, splitting a beer and watching the now-grown sheep in the field. On the days when it drizzled, they would go to the pub, chatting over a ploughman's lunch with brown bread, Cotswold Blue Brie, pickles, and a hard-boiled egg. Sometimes they'd curl up on the sofa in the den and watch a science fiction movie. It had never really been one of her genres, but Aaron was slowly convincing her that there was more than *Star Trek* and *Star Wars* that were worth watching.

She brushed a hand over the few leaves peeking out from the rose branches to cheer them on, then went inside and took her time cleaning up from the garden.

Ages ago, a lifetime ago, Aaron had said that he had some special ideas on how to christen the upstairs office when it was done. True to his word, he'd left it until last.

After a quick shower, she dressed. Before heading upstairs, she unwrapped the outfit she'd purchased for the occasion on her last trip up to London—a transaction that had embarrassed her and amused the perfectly polite English clerk. As she dressed for him, she felt a little wild, and very un-Jane-like...which maybe was a good thing. When she arrived at the door and leaned up against the jamb in the best pose she could manage, she wasn't sure which of them was more surprised.

The office was perfect. He'd found an old wooden roll-top desk that made her feel as if she'd just stepped back a century or two. A low bookcase, frilly curtains at both the garden window and the new one that looked out the other side of the cottage toward the spring itself. Instead of paint, he'd selected a pale, floral wallpaper that complimented the armchair she'd purchased so long ago. It was, a hazy memory finally came clear, the wallpaper that she'd noticed on that very first night as he'd walked a half-drunk woman through town. And he'd remembered that she'd liked it.

"Oh, Aaron!" It was perhaps the most feminine space she'd ever been in. It wasn't over-the-top or ridiculously girly. He'd taken photos of the gamboling lambs, a pheasant, and a wide photo of her walking barefoot through the water up Brook Lane in Blockley, and had them framed. With the desk and the choice of art, it stated that here worked a powerful businessperson who was also pure woman. She knew she was pretty, but she'd never seen herself as feminine, not until this moment. "Such a gift!"

"I was thinking the same thing myself." He too had cleaned up, even wearing clean slacks and a button-down shirt, opened down just enough buttons to show off his beautiful chest. He was staring at her.

"You like?" She tried a model pose that felt moderately ridiculous, but it must have worked because his smile went electric.

She hadn't quite been able to face a teddy, but she'd actually liked the black lacy underwear and bra. Over it she wore an almost sheer, white silk robe that barely reached the top of her thighs. After some trials in the mirror, she'd left it open in the front with the belt dangling loosely to either side rather than closing it or tying the sash across her bare stomach.

"You're not the only one who has been looking forward to this moment," she informed him.

"I can see that." He pointed to her armchair. "Sit."

"That wasn't quite the welcome I was expecting."

His groan of frustration was satisfying enough that she decided to humor him. However, to punish him for not sweeping her into his arms, she closed the robe as she sat. She made a point of admiring the view out the window rather than looking at her beautiful man and wondering just what he had in mind. Thankfully, it was an easy view to admire. The newly planted roses below, the pristine rock wall with its amazing arch that opened out onto the world, and in the distance the rolling hills that were the outer reaches of Fosse Manor.

"Close your eyes."

She did.

He walked around the room for a moment.

"How long do I keep them—"

"Just keep them closed, all right?" The frustration was oddly satisfying.

"Yes, sir!" Jane made a mock salute.

More walking around and then he stopped close beside her.

"Let me know if I hurt you."

"What—"

But her question was cut off in wonder as he gathered up some of her hair and ran a brush through it. She'd never had a man brush her hair before. Never had anyone, other than during a haircut, brushed it for her.

At first it felt awkward, even uncomfortable. But Aaron was gentle. She could remember him watching her each night as she started at the ends to clear tangles, then worked her way up until she could make long, smooth strokes through her hair. He gained confidence as he worked. Soon she was looking forward to each brushstroke. It was as if Aaron himself was caressing her, telling her how beautiful she was, how worthy she was. Every passage of the brush pulled joy from deeper and deeper until it was welling up out of her heart.

"I love you, Aaron Mason."

"I love you, Jane Tully." He didn't say it often, but she'd learned to cherish it each time he did. He was more of a show than tell kind of guy.

She gave herself to sensation as he worked his way around until her hair was far beyond any mere hundred strokes. She floated in a glorious space halfway between smiling and swooning.

When he finally stopped, she was floating in her chair.

"This is what you thought of, that day?"

"Yes."

"Brushing my hair."

"Uh-huh."

"Aaron?"

"Uh-huh?"

"Never stop thinking, okay?"

"Thinking about you? My favorite occupation. Now open your eyes."

It was hard. It was like coming back from some distant, fairy-tale land where reality had no place. When she finally forced her eyes open, she was looking once more at the green hills out the window.

In the center of the window ledge a star shone almost too brightly to look at.

She blinked her eyes trying to understand how Aaron had installed this bit of the sun in her office.

Then the world shifted.

A diamond ring, glowing with the afternoon sunlight.

Aaron reached out and picked it up. Then he knelt in front of her and offered it up to her.

"I know it's for tomorrow, but I didn't want to share the moment of giving it to you with anyone else."

"Tomorrow we will marry," she said as she held out her hand.

Aaron, her very own White Knight, slipped the ring onto her finger.

"Today," she smiled at the man who was the view of the wonder of her future. "Today we are wed."

"Forever," Aaron agreed.

Jane nodded, "Forever."

EPILOGUE

Jane tried to remember the woman who had stalked into this pub such a short time ago, but nothing fit. Three months and a lifetime's worth of change had happened since she'd been that woman. The person desperately seeking drunken oblivion to get her through her sister's wedding was a distant memory, almost an illusion.

Instead of being stared at by a dusty stranger, this evening the love of her life held the door for her to go through. His simplest caress, his palm against the small of her back as they headed for the bar, the warm surety that was Aaron's presence in her life. The small cottage on the Spanish coast had been a heavenly spot to honeymoon, but it felt so good to be back, in this town, in this place where it had all begun.

What she would now call a "strapping lad" stood at the bar, though she didn't recognize him. Hal must have just hired him.

"A pint of Guinness and another of the Donnington Gold," Aaron placed their order, then pointed to their usual table by the fire. "In for dinner. We'll be over there." His speech was still as efficient and to the point as ever. Jane now also knew that it was strategic. He'd probably scanned and assessed every person coming along the sidewalk and estimated how many were likely to be coming in. If they wanted their favorite table, they'd best grab it quickly.

"I'll bring them across," the man's words followed them as they passed others. Trent nodded a gruff welcome from the table where he hunkered with several other old-timers, all busy with baskets of whitebait and chips. Gwyneth the butcher—her living room would be their very first job—waved with her half-finished pint. They might be forever "The Americans" but they were also locals now. Bought in. With a business. Here to stay.

"Do you have any idea how wonderful that sounds?" Jane asked Aaron as he held her seat for her.

"How what sounds?"

"Here to stay. I thought you could read my mind."

"Other way around, *mi amor*. You're the mind reader on this team." He eased down with his back to the wall, facing the room, just the way he liked it. "Besides, 'Here to stay' never sounded like me, but some amazing woman convinced me I was wrong."

Jane was very amused that Aaron could say he loved her in Spanish far more comfortably than English. It was the only bit of Spanish (other than: please, thank you, and bathroom) that he'd picked up during their week abroad. Abroad because Fosse-on-the-Wold was now home.

She reached out to hold his hand as a cheery blonde delivered their beers and a pair of menus.

"Is Bridget off tonight?"

The blonde squinted at her, "Bridget?"

"Bridget..." but Jane didn't have a last name. She'd always just been Bridget.

"Can't say as I know who you mean," the blonde's accent was musically Welsh, so pleasant to listen to that it took Jane a moment to sort it out. Then the words registered.

"But—" Her throat went dry.

Aaron's hand twitched hard in hers.

"There's just me and Malcolm," the waitress pointed to the bartender, "if'n you don't be counting my sister and Ma doing the cooking."

"But—" the tightness in Jane's throat clamped off any more words.

Aaron squeezed her hand hard enough to get her attention, then he nodded toward the fireplace. It took her a moment to see what was wrong. In place of Snoop's doggy pillow there was now a booth, that looked as if it had been there since the place had opened a thousand years before. The Snoop Doggy Dogg statuette was gone from the mantle as well—a mantle that was too narrow to have ever held it.

She looked about the room. There were a hundred small differences that no one seemed to notice. Rather than dried hops hanging from the ceiling, there were small bundles of lavender. The stairway to the two rooms was gone, the stone wall seamless across the passage she and Aaron had traversed so many times.

"Oi. You must be that smashing American couple who're locals now. Certainly look it. Hang on," and the waitress hurried back toward the bar.

Jane could only look at Aaron in desperation. Something had shifted and she didn't understand it.

He had that intent hunting-falcon look that came over him when he was thinking hardest. Tracking, analyzing, he scanned the room. But she could see that he was finding no more answers than she was.

Then he tapped the menu.

She looked down.

It was just as aged and well-worn as ever, but the offerings were different. Traditional, but definitely not the same, except for her first meal of whitebait and chips.

He tapped it again, at the top.

"The *King's* Guard? But we were only gone for a week."

"Or maybe we were never here," Aaron's whisper did nothing to reassure her.

The waitress returned with a manila envelope. "Here you go. Elderly chap, very posh, brought this by a couple-a days back and said to give it to the 'smashing American couple' when they come in. Figure that must be you two. Be right back. I see an order's just come up."

Aaron took the envelope, which was good. Her own hands weren't working at the moment. She could feel herself hyperventilating and was doing her best to hold the panic at bay.

He inspected the contents, then handed across a very official-looking form. She had to blink several times to focus on the words. It was a vehicle title to the bronze MINI Cooper. It was in her name.

"We *were* here. But here isn't *here* anymore." She wasn't making any sense, even to herself, but she somehow knew she was right.

Aaron started to read the letter that had been in with it.

"*You said you didn't want the pink Ferrari.*"

"Conrad." Jane didn't know whether to laugh or cry. He, too, must be gone.

Aaron kept reading though she could hear how tight his voice was. He read fast as if he feared the letter itself might disappear before he finished it.

"*I hope I was right at taking you at your word and gifting you the MINI for your wedding instead—in truth a much more practical vehicle in any regards. Your cottage is paid off as well, it seemed the least I could make Geoffrey do. They also have reimbursed the money you put down, in recompense for all of the trouble Debbie caused you with the various bureaucracies. Seems they had quite the row over it as he hadn't known what she was up to—or so he claimed. I made it clear that they don't dare trouble you again or they shall be disinherited—apparently the only type of threat either can understand and a fate neither would risk.*"

"The cottage?"

Aaron only shrugged but she could read his relief in the

nuanced movement. No more battles. No tight pinch of fear. With the mortgage paid, they'd have time to grow their company now the way it should be. And free of Debbie? That was too big to think about now.

"Knowing the two of you has been a true joy. I would leave you my number should you ever need assistance, but I know you both will find all you need in the person sitting beside you and in this town you have grown to love. I have been called abroad and should I return, know that I will look in on you. Conrad"

"Do you think the manor is still there?" It was a crazy question.

Aaron squinted over at the booth again. "If it is, we might not recognize it. Or at least not know the people."

"What does it all mean? Hal, Bridget, Conrad?"

Aaron folded the letter carefully and handed it to her.

The paper felt real. At least that much remained.

He looked around the room and she followed his gaze. There was laughter at the bar and around the pub. Locals and tourists mixed as they always did. Two women sat down at the booth that was there now but never had been before. One of them had a beautiful golden retriever who inspected Jane briefly with his soulful eyes before settling happily at his mistress' feet.

Outside the leaded glass window, Fosse-on-the-Wold still bustled with life, vibrant without being hurried. Across the way, a family peered through the tea room's front window, then went inside. A large tractor drove through town pulling a massive trailer of hay as quickly as if he was alone on an open field. The usual swarm of cars and vans squeezed aside to accommodate him on the medievally-narrow road, then hurried on their way as soon as it was clear.

Just as she was turning back to face Aaron, a hot-pink Ferrari flashed down the street. She didn't manage a good look, only enough to know it wasn't her sister in the passenger seat. She had the oddest feeling that it was actually Hal. Perhaps with Bridget driving? She couldn't be sure, then a King Charles Spaniel stuck its head out the car's window and into the wind. Jane wondered if Hal was finally wearing his red Ferrari tie.

She turned back at Aaron.

"It's still home," she whispered.

"As long as you're here with me, it always will be," he nodded with that perfect certainty of his that always made her feel every-thing was right with the world. And, however impossibly, it was.

She'd finally found her heart in England and, by the pressure of Aaron's firm grip, she knew that was but one of so many precious things she'd never lose again.

COMING THIS WINTER:

PATH OF LOVE: ITALY

LOVE ABROAD B&B ROMANCE NOVEL #2

(*Via dell'Amore*)
Coming this winter

Erica was so done with being done with Dwayne. She was even done with being done with being…

Yep! There was the crazy loop that her head had been stuck in for, she did her best not to sigh at herself, far too long. Enough was enough, as all but her closest friends were nice enough *not* to say. And her closest friends—she'd come near enough to chasing them away altogether.

She sat on the grassy verge of the road, hugged her knees up against her chest, and tried not to look out at the idyllic Italian olive grove perched on the scenic hillside, backed by the vast Mediterranean and the blue sky that looked so perfect that it was easy to imagine the Roman gods still lived there.

So she had come to the land of love. And since she no longer believed in love, Erica decided that it was perhaps the dumbest decision she'd made in a long line of them.

She *had* always been curious about the Italian coast. Not the famous Amalfi stretch featured in every film since Hollywood directors had first discovered it in the 1950s. No, it was the small coastal towns to the north that she'd always imagined visiting. Ones where the bare bones of history lay upon the hillsides in thousand-year-old churches. Bridges and towers that had inspired Monet and Van Gogh. Especially the little piazzas where she could sit and watch the world walk by in its elegant, Italian fashion while sipping an espresso with—

But she'd come here alone.

And that *wasn't* the Italy she'd found.

She crouched at the edge of some impossible switchback, staring down over the scrub-brush edge of the crazy path down the steep hillside—a path carved by the tires of her rental car.

She'd missed the curve and had plunged fifty feet down the slope through the orchard.

The car had caromed off two aged olive trees, which had slowed her descent from dramatic to really annoying. Its final resting place against the granddaddy of the orchard was good enough for her. Stomped-on brakes and good fortune had lessened the impact enough that the air bag hadn't needed to deploy, though she could still feel the harsh line of the seatbelt across her chest.

She'd left the car there and climbed back up to the roadside, but there was no one to flag for help on the cliff-side road. Her cell phone was still down there in the car. So, she sat and glared at it for lack of anything better to do.

Italian drivers were crazy, but she'd watched enough television travel shows to be ready for that. Tailgaters? No prob. She'd grown up driving in LA. Manic passing? Nothing a Boston pro wouldn't try as she'd learned when life had led her there.

It was the Italian roads themselves she wasn't ready for. Narrow two lanes the size of a US back-country road were the major thoroughfares of the country. Only the massive Autostrade toll roads had multiple lanes, which were still painfully narrow. As she'd come here to see the countryside not the highways, she'd taken to the secondary highways at the first opportunity.

Along with every massive truck in the entire country.

The driving was narrow, fast, and terrifying.

Had been. She definitely wasn't getting back behind the wheel for as long as she was in Italy. The car could *rot* right where it was for all she cared.

And she was probably in shock, having just survived her descent into the olive grove. Could you tell when you were in shock or not, or did someone else have to tell you? By being able to ask the question, did that mean she wasn't in shock? Or that she was?

Or that she was losing her mind? Which wasn't really in doubt at the moment—she *definitely* was.

The gray-green leaves from where the orchard continued up above her filtered the hot Mediterranean sun of May into dappled laser beams among cool bits of shade. Leaves no bigger than her pinkie clustered and overlapped so tightly that she could barely see the white car down the cliff-like slope. Beneath the trees, grass thick with dandelions sought the sunny gaps.

Maybe she should sit...except she already was. She rested her forehead on her knees.

Ironically, it wasn't the two-lane "highway" with its massive trucks and speeding cars that had defeated her. Instead it had been this isolated one-lane road that wouldn't have been considered a decent driveway back home. According to her map, this narrow, switchbacked, and paved *goat trail* was the main road into her randomly chosen destination, the tiny town Riva Lontana perched above the Ligurian coast. One blink of inattention, a pair of motorcycles racing up the hill as she'd descended, and she'd plunged off the edge.

"Perfect metaphor for your life, Erica."

So she squatted on the verge and stared at the impossibly blue sky over the miraculously blue sea and wondered how hard it would be to get back to the nearest airport and just go home.

But there was the car. She should at least let someone know it was there. Maybe someone who could just make it so that it had never happened. The car. The flight to Italy. Leaving Boston. Sleeping with her boss, her *married* boss, so full of promises and lies.

How had she been so naive? So…desperate?

Erica double-checked that her little traffic triangle was perched on the road's edge behind her. "Every Italian car," the rental agent had told her as if it was the most important secret to driving in Italy, "has reflective triangle. Must use if in, ah, *incidente.*"

It was the only remaining bit of control in her life, placing that foot-high warning triangle beside her on the edge of the road.

Danger! Here sits a disaster of a woman. Approach at your own risk.

Better yet: *For your own safety, stay clear of this woman!*

Since her car was off the road, its nose crumpled against a massive tree, she figured it counted as an *incidente.* Her pack was still down there somewhere. Her cell phone too. But, by god, her little red reflective triangle was on the road where it should be.

A smooth, dangerous sound behind her had her turning in time to see a hot pink Ferrari slide to a stop close behind her. A cheery brunette, whose dark hair spilled down over her shoulders, leaned out of the car.

"Are you all right, *tesoro?*"

"*Tesoro?*"

"*Chérie.* My friend. You do not look happy." The brunette offered her a pout of sympathy.

"I've had better days," she pointed down-slope at her car. An elderly gentleman had come from somewhere in the trees and was inspecting the disaster.

The woman strained to peer over the edge of the drop-off.
And giggled.

"Your car?"

"Rental."

"And you are not hurt?"

Other than her pride, her soul, her… Erica shook her head no.

"Oh. Everything is okay then."

"How do you figure that?"

The brunette climbed out of the blazingly pink Ferrari. She was tall and generously built. She wore simple Italian chic of silk blouse, tight jeans, and stylish boots that Erica always wanted but could never seem to find. The light leather jacket looked to be for effect rather than warmth. A woman in her prime. Much of Italy struck her that way, which made her want to stamp "Warning: Dowdy American" on her forehead to tell them to stay clear.

A rotund brown-and-white spaniel followed her and came over to sniff at Erica's hand. It appeared immune to the triangular warning sign, so she petted it. The dog sighed happily, so she petted it some more. The first thing to go right with her day.

"I'm called Brigitte. He's named Snoop. And I am guessing that you need a place to stay."

"Well, I'm thinking that I shouldn't leave town until that is dealt with."

"Oh pfft!" Brigitte waved a hand at the car as if it was of no consequence.

"Shouldn't I contact the police or something?"

"Corrado can take care of that for us, can't you, darling?"

Erica turned to see that the man who had been inspecting her car had climbed the hill carrying her pack. He handed it and her cell phone over very solemnly. He was an older gentleman who looked to be far above such menial tasks.

"Is that your tree?"

"They all are," his smile was unexpectedly easy and made his blue-gray eyes practically twinkle. "You have parked your conveyance in my olive orchard."

"I'm terribly sorry. Let me know if there is any damage. I'll repay it..." *somehow.* She was an unanchored craft in the storm that was her life. It wasn't as if she had some deep bankroll to survive whatever was happening to her.

"These trees have been standing since long before the Medici first rose to power in the 1400s. They have seen far worse than your *piccolo macchina.* I shall call Marceto and see that it is returned where it must go. Would you like a replacement?"

"Not on your life," Erica blushed. "Sorry, but no thanks."

"*É finito!*" He snapped his fingers as if he could work magic.

"Henri?" Brigitte was talking into a cell phone. "Do we have a room open? *Sì? Perfetto!* I will be home soon and bringing a guest."

The woman stepped up and kissed Corrado on both cheeks.

Was Erica supposed to do the same? Unsure of herself, she held out a hand. He bent over it and placed a kiss on the back of her hand like a gentleman of old.

"Oh, Corri, you old hound," Brigitte teased him, but Erica felt touched. "We must find another woman for you. Your wife is long gone now, rest her soul."

"She will have to be a very special one," his smile teased that she must be just like Erica. *As if.* Besides, he was at least twice her age, maybe closer to three times, though he'd carried her pack very easily.

"Come! We have a most charming B&B. You must see it. You will never want to leave."

Erica's pack filled the Ferrari's tiny trunk. She slid into the leather passenger seat, which felt even better than first class looked after a twelve-hour flight in coach. She pulled on her seatbelt, barely in time. Snoop climbed up to sit on her lap and rest his chin on the door.

The engine roared to life, Brigitte flashed a wave to Corrado, who waved a solemn hand in reply from his olive trees. The

Ferrari leapt forward, slamming her back into the seat as they raced down the narrow twisting street she'd barely been creeping along. Snoop leaned his side into her chest and she wrapped an arm around him as his ears flapped out in the wind.

She was in the hands of strangers and had no idea what came next.

ABOUT THE AUTHOR

M.L. Buchman started the first of, what is now over 50 novels and as many short stories, while flying from South Korea to ride his bicycle across the Australian Outback. Part of a solo around the world trip that ultimately launched his writing career.

All three of his military romantic suspense series—The Night Stalkers, Firehawks, and Delta Force—have had a title named "Top 10 Romance of the Year" by the American Library Association's *Booklist*. NPR and Barnes & Noble have named other titles "Top 5 Romance of the Year." In 2016 he was a finalist for Romance Writers of America prestigious RITA award. He also writes: contemporary romance, thrillers, and fantasy.

Past lives include: years as a project manager, rebuilding and single-handing a fifty-foot sailboat, both flying and jumping out of airplanes, and he has designed and built two houses. He is now making his living as a full-time writer on the Oregon Coast with his beloved wife and is constantly amazed at what you can do with a degree in Geophysics. You may keep up with his writing and receive a free starter e-library by subscribing to his news-letter at: www.mlbuchman.com

Join the conversation:
www.mlbuchman.com

ALSO BY M. L. BUCHMAN

THE NIGHT STALKERS

MAIN FLIGHT

The Night Is Mine

I Own the Dawn

Wait Until Dark

Take Over at Midnight

Light Up the Night

Bring On the Dusk

By Break of Day

WHITE HOUSE HOLIDAY

Daniel's Christmas

Frank's Independence Day

Peter's Christmas

Zachary's Christmas

Roy's Independence Day

Damien's Christmas

AND THE NAVY

Christmas at Steel Beach

Christmas at Peleliu Cove

5E

Target of the Heart

Target Lock on Love

Target of Mine

FIREHAWKS

Main Flight
Pure Heat
Full Blaze
Hot Point
Flash of Fire
Wild Fire
Smokejumpers
Wildfire at Dawn
Wildfire at Larch Creek
Wildfire on the Skagit

Delta Force
Main Flight
Target Engaged
Heart Strike
Wild Justice

Henderson's Ranch
Nathan's Big Sky

Love Abroad B&B
Heart of the Cotswolds: England

Where Dreams
Where Dreams are Born
Where Dreams Reside
Where Dreams Are of Christmas
Where Dreams Unfold
Where Dreams Are Written

EAGLE COVE

Return to Eagle Cove

Recipe for Eagle Cove

Longing for Eagle Cove

Keepsake for Eagle Cove

DEITIES ANONYMOUS

Cookbook from Hell: Reheated

Saviors 101

DEAD CHEF

Swap Out!

One Chef!

Two Chef!

SF/F TITLES

The Nara Reaction

Monk's Maze

The Me and Elsie Chronicles

STRATEGIES FOR SUCCESS

Managing Your Inner Artist / Writer

Don't miss a thing! Get a free starter library!

www.mlbuchman.com